THE
INTERNATIONAL JEWISH
SPORTS HALL OF FAME

THE
INTERNATIONAL JEWISH
SPORTS HALL OF FAME

Joseph M. Siegman

Foreword by Mark Spitz

S.P.I. BOOKS

A division of Shapolsky Publishers, Inc.

For additional information, contact:
S.P.I. BOOKS/Shapolsky Publishers, Inc.
136 West 22nd Street
New York, NY 10011
(212) 633-2022   FAX (212) 633-2123

10 9 8 7 6 5 4 3 2 1

ISBN 1-56171-028-8

Design by Sherrel Farnsworth
Typography by Smith Inc., New York
Manufactured in the United States of America

INTERNATIONAL JEWISH SPORTS HALL OF FAME

*"The deeds of the past
shall inspire
the achievements
of the future."*

ACKNOWLEDGMENTS

Much of the material in this book has been gathered over twelve years—not for inclusion in a publication, but rather to conduct the various selection processes of the International Jewish Sports Hall of Fame. Therefore, expressions of gratitude to the following sources of information come not only from the author, but also from all those involved in the development and management of the IJSHOF.

No single individual has been more important to the IJSHOF's collection of records, background stories, and photographs than Dr. Uriel Simri. He has been particularly effective in acquiring details and records of European athletes and sportsmen whose outstanding achievements were performed long before statistics became a science.

No single publication has been a more treasured research tool for the IJSHOF than *The Encyclopedia of Jews in Sports,* published in 1965 by Bloch Publishing, New York, and written by Jesse Silver, Roy Silver, and Bernard Postal. The *Encyclopedia* is a masterpiece of research and detail, presenting both cold facts and fascinating narratives on its worldwide subjects. Another invaluable aid was Robert Slater's *Great Jews in Sports,* published by Jonathan David Publishers, Middle Village, New York, in 1983. The Slater book provides a contemporary accounting of American sportsmen, and also devotes special sections to Israeli sport figures, as well as to the Macccabiah Games.

Over the years, information needed for the IJSHOF has been gathered from many publications. Significant among them were: Bill Henry's *An Approved History of the Olympic Games* (Los Angeles: Southern California Committee for the Olympic Games, 1981); Harold Ribalow's *The Jew in American Sports* (New York: Bloch Publishing, 1948, 1954, rev. 1955, 1966; Hippocrene Books, 1985); the section on sports in the *Encyclopedia Judaica* (various editions); *Ring Magazine Record Book & Boxing Encyclopedia,* ed. Herbert G. Goldman (New York: The Ring Publishing Co.); and Chaim Wein's *The Maccabiah Games in Eretz Israel* (Maccabi World Union and Wingate Institute for Physical Education and Sport, Israel).

Countless individuals have contributed to the background knowledge of the athletes and sportsmen enshrined in the IJSHOF. Both Dr. Simri and this author have enjoyed personal contact with many of the Hall of Fame honorees. Families of both living and deceased honored athletes and sportsmen have contributed greatly to the information gathered by the IJSHOF, as have colleges, professional sport franchises, sports associations and other halls of fame.

Perhaps the most challenging task has been acquiring photos of each of our honorees. Diligent and often relentless research by the following resources has provided most of the photo art displayed in the International Jewish Sports Hall of Fame Museum and pictured in this book: Shlomo Korlandchik, Wingate Institute Photo Archives, Netanya, Israel; Eliezer Shmueli, Nahum Goldman Museum of the Diaspora–Beth Hatefusoth, Tel Aviv University, Israel; Arthur Hanak, Pierre Gildesgame Museum, Maccabi World Union, Ramat Gan, Israel; and Wayne Wilson, Shirley Ito, and Braven Dyer, Jr., Amateur Athletic Foundation (and its predecessors), Los Angeles, California.

For their assistance in providing information and/or photographs for this book, I would especially like to thank: Wayne Patterson at the Naismith Memorial Basketball Hall of Fame, Springfield, Massachusetts; Marion Washburn at the International Swimming Hall of Fame, Fort Lauderdale, Florida; Cheryl Rielly at the Canada Sports Hall of Fame, Toronto, Ontario; Al Cartwright and the International Association of Halls of Fame and Museums; the Detroit Tigers Baseball Club, Detroit, Michigan; the Sports Information Department, University of Michigan, Ann Arbor; the Department of Athletics, University of Pittsburgh, Pittsburgh, Pennsylvania; Syracuse University, Syracuse, New York; Norm Shindler, University of California at Los Angeles; the South African Embassy, Beverly Hills, California; Philip Redman of the York Barbell Company, York, Pennsylvania; San Antonio Spurs, San Antonio, Texas; Lee Snyder of the University of North Carolina, Chapel Hill; the Los Angeles Turf Club, Arcadia, California; Vern Roberts, United States Handball Association, Tucson, Arizona; Jordan Kurnick, *Nor-Mar News,* Chatsworth, California; the International Motor Sports Hall of Fame, Talladega, Alabama; Fred Grossman, Daily Racing Form, Inc., Heightstown, New Jersey; Harold Esch, Mount Dora, Florida; and Mort Rimer, Multiple Photos, Inc.

Special thanks go to: Israel's Beth Hatefusoth, on the campus of Tel Aviv University, for permission to reprint Dr. Uriel Simri's historical perspective,

Jews in the World of Sports; publisher Alan Hahn, Los Angeles, for his counsel, guidance, and efforts; Sol Marshall, Van Nuys, California, a resourceful contributor; John Monteleone, Mountain Lion, Inc., Rocky Hill, New Jersey, for efforts in organizing the book project; Zipora Seidner, Public Relations Director, Wingate Institute, a steady hand and coordinator of IJSHOF activities; Judah Rand-Lakritz, Wingate Institute, IJSHOF Executive Secretary; Michael Siegman, Beverly Hills, California, tireless provider of technical resources; Donn Teal, caring and patient editor; and Alan Sherman, Bethesda, Maryland, mentor and energy source.

Joseph M. Siegman

CONTENTS

THE PILLAR OF ACHIEVEMENT

—————————

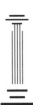

FOREWORD

It seems remarkable that Jewish men and women can reach the highest levels of success in such areas as medicine, science, law, and the arts, with little to no notice paid to their religious heritage, while a successful Jewish athlete is celebrated nearly as much for being a Jew as he or she is for their competitive accomplishments. To many, particularly Jews themselves, the Jewish athlete is a novelty.

Facts belie the misconception. In the past one hundred years, Jews have played a significant role in sports—both in participation and in sports development. As this wonderful book underscores, early athletes, such as England's Daniel Mendoza, began a long line of Jewish world boxing champions; Canada's Louis Rubenstein and Hungary's Lily Kronberger pioneered world figure skating; America's Lipman Pike was so good that he was *paid* to play for his baseball team—becoming the first-ever professional ball player; John Brunswick and his family pioneered billiards and tenpin bowling; nine gold medals were won by Jewish athletes at the first modern Olympic Games, in 1896; and today's National Basketball Association owes its origins to Jewish players, coaches, and entrepreneurs. The list of Jewish contributions to sports, past and present, on and off the field of play, is immense.

There is merit in the observation that Jews have not made big names for themselves in sports *in great numbers*, at least not the kind of numbers that our people have enjoyed in other careers and professions. Nevertheless, if we have over-achieved in some areas, the fact that we have merely succeeded in sports in proportion to our numbers doesn't make us under-achievers.

Without doubt, sociological and traditional elements have played an important role in the Jew's involvement in sports. But, then, haven't these same elements played similar roles in the participation of non-Jews in sports, as well? There are simply fewer Jews in the equation.

Following the 1972 Olympics, I recall one writer labeling me "the first great Jewish athlete." A compliment was intended, but the statement was hardly accurate. Long before there was a Mark Spitz, in American sports alone there was a Koufax, a Greenberg, a Ross, a Leonard, a Holman, a Luckman, and so many others! I may have been the Jewish champion of the moment, but many great athletes preceded me, and some have already succeeded me. Anyone with doubts about this need only thumb through the pages of this fascinating book. More than 150 of the world's all-time greatest athletes and contributors to sports are chronicled in these pages. And all of them are Jewish. Every one of those pictured in this book represents the best of his sport, and the best of his era. I am honored to be counted among these remarkable people.

Mark Spitz
Los Angeles, California
1992

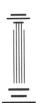

INTRODUCTION

This is a book that chronicles many of the world's greatest athletes and sportsmen. All of them are Jewish, and each is an elected member of the International Jewish Sports Hall of Fame. Some of the honorees date back to the late 18th century, although most are of the 20th. Not all are famous. But all were/are great sportsmen and women—Olympic champions, world record holders, professional all-stars, and others who have made extraordinary contributions to the world of sports.

Interior of the museum of the International Jewish Sports Hall of Fame at the Wingate Institute, Netanya, Israel. In the center can be seen the Pillar of Faith, holding the names of the eleven athletes killed by terrorists at the 1972 Munich Olympic Games. At far right is the Piero Brolis Sculpture, donated to the IJSHOF in 1982, which also honors the Munich Eleven.

A museum visitor views the display commemorating the achievements of American Olympic swimming champion Mark Spitz.

The concept of a Jewish Sports Hall of Fame was conceived, appropriately, on an El Al flight returning from the July 1977 Maccabiah Games in Israel. A group of Los Angeles-area athletes, competitors in the Games, and "high" on the inspirational enthusiasm one feels following the combination of exhilaration and exhaustion, wanted to find some way of letting American Jewry know more about its best-kept secret: the Maccabiah Games. A Hall of Fame was their idea. Let the famous names of Jewish sports stars of the past call attention to the activities of Jewish sports stars of the future.

A committee of four—Wilbur "Bud" Gold, Mike Kolsky, Ron Solomon, and myself—met on several occasions, developed a presentation to the United States Committee Sports for Israel (sponsors of the American

Maccabiah Team), and within a short time were given the green light to proceed with our plan.

Our electors were to be the 56 directors of the USCSFI, a group that included sports writers, coaches, former outstanding amateur and professional athletes, and active sportsmen. But the difficult part was the ballot. Who would be on the ballot? Having decided upon having 18 individuals as our first honorees—18 for "Chai"—where in the world were we going to come up with 18 superstar Jewish athletes to elect? We were well-versed, of course, on the accomplishments of Koufax and Greenberg, Leonard and Ross, Luckman and Goldberg, Mark Spitz, a few professional coaches, and some college and professional players who were more notable for being Jewish athletes rather than great athletes. But we wanted 18 greats—by anyone's standards.

Our ignorance quickly dissipated. After a sojourn with the excellent sports volume of the *Encyclopedia Judaica* and a reading of Harold Ribalow's *The Jew in American Sports* (New York: Bloch Publishing, 1948; Hippocrene, 1985), we encountered the monumental *Encyclopedia of Jews in Sports,* by Bernard Postal, Roy Silver, and Jesse Silver (New York: Bloch Publishing, 1966). It was the dawning of a new age for us. Finding 18 great Jewish athletes was no longer the problem. Who would be pared off our list to make the 36 on our first ballot was the new consideration! To our delight (and surprise), every ballot mailed was quickly returned—all completed, many with accompanying notations of praise for the Hall of Fame idea, as well as names of possible future candidates. We were now pressed into the next step of our plan: a dinner to honor those elected.

The inaugural dinner of the Jewish Sports Hall of Fame was held on Sunday, May 20, 1979, at the Los Angeles Beverly Hilton Hotel. Attending honorees were Red Auerbach, Jackie Fields, Hank Greenberg, Nat Holman, Jimmy Jacobs, Irving Jaffee, Sid Luckman, Dolph Schayes, Dick Savitt, and Sylvia Wene. Also on hand were family members representing deceased honorees Hirsch Jacobs, Benny Leonard, Barney Ross, and Abe Saperstein.

It was the greatest gathering ever of Jewish sports stars on one dais, and likely one of the most remarkable sports daises of any kind. Comedian Dick Shawn was master of ceremonies, with presenters including entertainers Milton Berle, Elliott Gould, Jack Carter, Shelley Berman, and Pat Henry. Israel's revered sports hero Tal Brody was a special guest, as were other prominent sportsmen nominated by the honorees as their presenters. Many other sports stars were in attendance as former teammates and/or close friends of the honorees, in addition to an impressive group of media people. It was quite a night for the guests of honor, as well as the 400 guests who attended the gala affair.

With that first dinner/induction evening, a new posture arose for what was originally conceived primarily to call attention to the Maccabiah Games. People were interested in a Jewish Sports Hall of Fame. Athletes and sportsmen who had received every honor their sport had to offer found it significant to be present and counted as the best of their own people. The media took to it, and support mail poured in, many of the letters relating stories of how the success of a Benny Leonard, or a Barney Ross or a Hank Greenberg had affected the writers' personal lives.

In Washington, D.C., Alan Sherman, a national vice-president of the USCSFI, and chairman of the 1977 USA Maccabiah Team (in overall charge of the entire American squad of 400 youngsters), and longtime activist in various and assorted U.S.–Israel activities, was convinced that the Jewish Sports Hall of Fame should have a home—a permanent museum in Israel. At his own expense, he ventured to Israel, scouted and negotiated several locations, and eventually determined that Israel's Wingate Institute, a personal project itself of the USCSFI, was the place to set anchor. Coincidentally, Wingate, at the time, was in the process of designing a new student union building, and the spacious foyer of its grand auditorium would be the perfect spot for the new Hall of Fame museum. Sherman undertook the task of raising $60,000 to complete the goal. He raised $135,000.

On July 27, 1980, once again at L.A.'s Beverly Hilton Hotel, the Second Annual Jewish Sports Hall of Fame Induction Dinner took place, this time some 500 guests packing the Grand Ballroom to honor attending sports legends: Mel Allen, Isaac Berger, Marshall Goldberg, Harry Litwack, Ron Mix, Al Rosen, and special honoree Gretel Bergmann (Mrs. Margaret Lambert). Family members representing deceased honorees were also in attendance, along with presenting entertainers George Jessel, Jack Carter, radio/TV newscaster Alex Drier, Los Angeles sports personality Bud Furillo, and L.A. Dodgers Vice-President Al Campanis. This wonderful evening was to be our last Americans-only induction/dinner gala.

Nearly one year later, on July 7, 1981, on the eve of the Eleventh World Maccabiah Games, Eliezer Shmueli, Director General of the Israel Ministry of Education and Physical Culture, and Honorary Chairman of the new International Jewish Sports Hall of Fame, cut the ceremonial ribbon signaling the opening of the new facility, the Hall of Fame Museum. At the time of its dedication, 47 names were entered into the attractive display cases that line the walls of the Hall. Ten years later, 157 individuals are held in honor. And, as it has since the day of the 1981 dedication, the Hall of Fame's Pillar of Faith marks the names of the 11 Israeli athletes murdered by Arab terrorists at the 1972 Olympic Games in Munich.

Two years in the United States and ten more in Israel, the International Jewish Sports Hall of Fame has stood as the clarion of honor for those Jewish athletes and sportsmen whose benchmark was excellence in their field. We have only just begun. We have recorded the past for future generations to emulate or surpass. The deeds of the past shall inspire the achievements of the future.

Joseph M. Siegman
Beverly Hills, California
1992

JEWS IN THE WORLD OF SPORTS:
A HISTORICAL VIEW
by Dr. Uriel Simri

The vicissitudes of fate experienced by the Jewish people in the modern era have inevitably led to too little attention being paid to many vital aspects of Jewish life. One such aspect is sports. Involvement in sports is universal throughout today's world. It serves as a bridge between nations and peoples...between nations and Israel...and between Israel and the Diaspora, as expressed by the Maccabiah Games. Physical culture and involvement in sport are among the fields that the Jewish people have entered in the modern era.

The end of the 18th century is seen as the dawning of the era of modern sport. Jews were already involved in athletic activities by that time. Among the top early boxers who made their appearance in the English sports arena were the Jews Samuel Elias, Barney Aaron, the Belasco brothers, and Isaac Bitton.

The best known among them was Daniel Mendoza, of Portuguese origin, who held the English boxing crown during the years 1794–95. Crowds of English fans came to see the brilliant boxing style of "Mendoza the Jew," as he proudly called himself. The numerous editorial cartoons and stories about Mendoza circulated in the press during that time spoke to his popularity, along with popular ditties that were composed in his honor. A source of pride to his people, Mendoza became the favorite of the English masses. Even the Prince of Wales was one of his notable fans. He is considered the

* Dr. Uriel Simri is one of the world's foremost educators and authorities on physical culture. Executive Director of the International Jewish Sports Hall of Fame from its inception in 1981 through 1989, Simri has been associated with Wingate Institute in various positions since 1966, including serving as its deputy director and scientific director. An international lecturer and governmental advisor, he is past-president of the Society for the History of Physical Education and Sport in Asia and was secretary/treasurer of the International Society for Comparative Physical Education and Sport.

England's Daniel Mendoza battles Richard Humphreys. The match was held on September 29, 1790.

father of "scientific boxing." As such, he transformed the sport from one of pure violence and brawn into an art and a "battle of wits."

In the second half of the 19th century, Jews such as Lipman Pike, Lon Myers, and Lewis Rubinstein were prominent figures among the elite in the world of sport. In 1866, Pike became America's first professional baseball player. Myers was the fastest runner in the world during the 1880s. And Canadian Rubinstein captured the first world title in figure-skating in 1890.

In the first half of the 20th century, many Jewish athletes turned to sports that demanded outstanding strength. Some explain this as an attempt to crush the image of the Jew as a weakling. Professional boxing, for example, brought young Jewish athletes high income and prestige, especially in the years preceding World War II. The list of world boxing champions in different

Lip Pike, born in New York City in 1845, played third base for the Philadelphia Athletics and would later become baseball's first professional player as well as its first homerun champion.

weight classes includes 29 Jewish boxers: 23 from the United States, 3 from France (North Africa), and 3 from Great Britain. The most outstanding among them were America's Benny Leonard and Barney Ross. Leonard held the World Lightweight title from 1917 to 1925, retiring undefeated. His countryman Barney Ross was World Champion in the lightweight as well as welterweight class in 1934 and 1935, and was the first boxer to ever hold two world titles simultaneously. In the amateur ranks, Jewish boxers and wrestlers, representing eight different countries, have won 18 Olympic medals. Many of those same athletes, as well as others, have captured numerous world titles.

Another sport in which Jews have excelled is fencing. Among the winners of Olympic medals and/or world titles in this sport are Jews from Austria,

Belgium, Great Britain, Denmark, the United States, Hungary, and France. Fencing has been considered a "Jewish sport" in the Soviet Union. Olympic gold medalists such as Mark Midler, Grigory Kriss, and Jacob Rylsky have brought considerable honor to that nation.

Jewish athletes have also enjoyed notable achievements in table tennis. The most famous Jewish table tennis player is Hungary's Viktor Barna, winner of 22 world titles during the 1930s. Second to Barna is Richard Bergmann, of Austria and Great Britain, winner of four world titles in the 1930s and 1950s. The Hungarian table tennis team, which held the World Championship eight times between 1927 and 1935, was composed almost entirely of Jewish players—as was the Austrian team that took the title from Hungary in 1936. In the years following World War II, Romania's Angelica Rozeanu was the most prominent Jewish figure in table tennis. Beginning in 1950, she won 17 world titles. (She currently resides in Israel.)

Members of the 1908 Hungarian gold-medal fencing team. Left to right: Lajos Werkner, Dr. Oszkar Gerde, and Dr. Jeno Fuchs.

*Basketball coaching legends
Harry Litwak (left) and
Nat Holman, at
Litwak's 1980 induction
into the Hall of Fame.
Holman had been
elected one year earlier.*

Among the ranks of outstanding Jewish basketball players and coaches in the United States are Nat Holman, Red Auerbach, Harry Litwack, Red Holzman, Dolph Schayes, and Max Zaslofsky. Major league baseball lore recalls the names Hank Greenberg, Sandy Koufax, and Al Rosen. And prominent among American football players, amateur and/or professional, are such Jewish stars as Sid Luckman, Benny Friedman, Marshall Goldberg, and Ron Mix, as well as coaches Sid Gillman, Marv Levy, and Al Davis.

The first modern Olympic Games were held in Athens in 1896. Athletes from throughout the world participated in these games, and there was a respectable representation of Jews among them. Five Jews won ten medals (eight golds): gymnast Alfred Flatow (Germany), three gold medals and one silver; gymnast Gustav Felix Flatow (Germany), Alfred's cousin, two gold medals; swimmer Alfred Hajos-Guttmann (Hungary), two gold medals;

swimmer Paul Neumann (Austria), one gold medal; and swimmer Otto Herschmann (Austria), one bronze medal. In 1912, Herschmann won a second Olympic medal, a silver, in fencing—the first athlete to receive Olympic medals in two different sports. In 1924, twenty-eight years after winning his two golds in swimming, Hajos-Guttmann received his third Olympic medal, a silver for designing sports facilities. (Silver was the highest honor presented in the design competition.)

Space does not permit enumeration of all the Jewish athletes who won medals in the 23 modern Olympic Games. Suffice it to say that Jews have been the recipients of nearly 250—more than 100 of them golds. The athlete who captured the greatest number of medals in any one Olympiad is American swimmer Mark Spitz. Spitz won seven gold medals at the Munich Games in 1972, setting new world records in each of his events (including three relay races). Four years earlier, at the Olympics in Mexico City, Spitz had won "only" two gold medals, one silver, and one bronze.

The most successful Jewish woman athlete to participate in the Olympics is Hungarian gymnast Agnes Keleti, a winner of eleven Olympic medals—five gold, four silver, and two bronze—in the Games of 1948, 1952, and 1956. (She has lived in Israel since 1957.)

Jews have not only been outstanding athletes; they have also figured prominently among the leaders of the wider sports world. As early as the eve of World War I, America's Charlotte Epstein fought successfully for the introduction of women's swimming events in the United States, and she stood at the helm of this sport in her country for many years. In the 1920s and 1930s, Hakoah-Vienna's "Wunderteam" of Austrian soccer was guided by the skillful hands of Hugo Meisl. And sports for the handicapped, which developed on an international scale after World War II, owes a debt of gratitude to its initiator, Sir Ludwig Guttmann, a German-Jewish doctor who fled to Britain during the war. These are just a few among many.

It was Max Nordau's call for the creation of a "new Jew" and for "muscular Judaism," at the 2nd World Zionist Congress in 1898, that marked the beginnings of a new awareness of physical culture among Jews, particularly in Europe. At the turn of the century, Jewish gymnastics clubs were established, encouraging thousands of Jewish youngsters to engage in physical exercise and serving as a framework for nationalistic activity.

As early as 1895, German Jews living in Constantinople had established the first Jewish gymnastics club after being expelled from the local, nationalistic German club. In 1897, a Jewish gymnastics club called Gibor (later changed to Samson) was founded in Phillipople, Bulgaria. While the Jewish club in Constantinople was created as a result of anti-Semitism, the one in Bulgaria was an expression of newly aroused Jewish national consciousness—following the example of Sokol, the national Slavic gymnastics movement. Anti-Semitism and Jewish nationalism, then, were responsible for the spread of the Jewish gymnastics movement.

Max Nordau's exhortation did not fall upon deaf ears. In 1898, the Bar Kochba Club was organized in Berlin, and within a short time, dozens of other Jewish gymnastics groups sprang up, primarily in German-speaking countries. This widespread activity resulted in the establishment, in 1903,

Members of Maccabi Bombay in 1931 display homemade Mogen Davids.

of the Jüdische Turnerschaft, an umbrella organization for Jewish gymnastics clubs. The gymnastics displays that members of the Turnerschaft performed for delegates of the 7th Zionist Congress in Basel, and for subsequent congresses, aroused emotion and pride. They were tangible evidence of the connection between Jewish physical culture and the Jewish national movement.

Following the German tradition, the first Jewish sports clubs were devoted solely to gymnastics. Beginning in 1906, however, broader-based sports clubs were also established. Hungarian Jews were pioneers in the field, establishing the VAC Club in Budapest that year. In 1909, the Hakoah Club of Vienna was born.

By the beginning of World War I, the Jewish athletic movement had spread to other European and Middle Eastern countries as well. Though the war closed many clubs, it also provided the impetus for the creation of new ones. A case in point is the Warsaw Club. The Russian rulers of this part of Poland had forbidden the organization of a Jewish athletic club, but the German invaders, in 1915, allowed Jews to form a Maccabi club. This was to be the largest Jewish athletic club in Europe during the period between the two world wars.

The political changes wrought by World War I led to the establishment of dozens of new Jewish sports clubs, and a new umbrella organization was created in 1921. This, the Maccabi World Union, united most of the Jewish athletic clubs. The regulations of the organization stated: "The goal of the Union is the physical and moral rejuvenation of Jews for the sake of restoration and existence of the Jewish land and people."

In the period between the two world wars, the activities of the Maccabi Union spread throughout the Jewish world, reaching as far as Australia, South America, and South Africa. The center of activity, nevertheless, remained in Europe in the form of hundreds of Maccabi clubs. Most prominent were the previously mentioned Hakoah Club of Vienna and the Hagibor Club of Prague, whose notable achievements in national and international track and field and swimming competitions aroused pride and identification among European Jewry. Greatest of all Jewish teams was the soccer team of Hakoah-Vienna, which held the Austrian championship in 1925. The best Jewish soccer players in Central Europe joined its ranks, bringing the team worldwide acclaim. Everywhere the club went—Europe, the United States, Eretz [the

Land of] Yisrael—it aroused enthusiasm and pride among fellow Jews.

In addition to athletic activities, the Maccabi clubs became the center of extensive cultural and social activities. They were more than merely sports organizations that promoted physical fitness—they also wielded considerable influence among Jewish communities.

The Maccabi Union was not the sole organization concerned with physical culture. During the 1930s, the Hapoel organization in Eretz Yisrael operated dozens of athletic clubs in the Diaspora, mainly in Poland, Lithuania, and Latvia. Despite prevailing political and financial limitations, they promoted numerous athletic and social events. Betar was also active in promoting sports for Jewish youth. The Betar clubs in China and Manchuria were outstanding both in the scope of their activities and in the quality of their athletic achievements. In addition to these avowedly Zionist frameworks, other Jewish athletic clubs should be mentioned: the clubs of the Bund in Poland, and those of Canada, as well as the network of sports facilities established in the magnificent Jewish community centers built by North American Jewry— centers that continue to flourish today.

INTERNATIONAL INTER CLUB **AQUATIC GALA**
SATURDAY 18th SEPT. 1937
MARYLEBONE   BATHS   W.
MACCABI   ASSOCIATION   LONDON   SWIMMING   CLUB.

A poster announces an international swimming and diving competition in 1937, organized by the London Maccabi Swimming Club.

Nordau's exhortation to rejuvenate "muscular Judaism" has fallen on fertile ground, indeed. Today in Israel, as well as in the Diaspora, sports have become an accepted endeavor for Jews of all classes and all ages. For athletes and fans alike, sports have become a focus of identification— and an integral part of our lives.

Perhaps the most idyllic of Max Nordeau's dreams, and certainly the greatest individual achievement in the history of the modern Olympic Games, was the winning of seven gold medals by American swimmer Mark Spitz in 1972. Spitz, here with his wife Susie, received his International Jewish Sports Hall of Fame award at a special ceremony on March 1983, in Beverly Hills, California.

AUTO RACING

JODY SCHECKTER
South Africa

Born January 29, 1950, in East London, South Africa

As Formula One World Champion in 1979, he was the first South African to win a World title. Scheckter joined the Formula One circuit in 1974, winning the British and Swedish Grand Prix. He placed third in the World Championship and was named Driver of the Year by the British Guild of Motoring Writers. In 1976, he again finished third in the World Championship rankings. The following year, Scheckter was runner-up in his quest for the World title, with triumphs in Argentina, Monaco, and Canada. In 1979, following wins in the Belgian, Monaco, and Italian Grand Prix, he captured the World Formula One Racing Car Championship.

Prior to entering the Grand Prix circuit, Scheckter was a prominent stock car racer in his native South Africa, graduating to Formula Ford and Formula Two racing in the early 1970s. In 1972, he won the American Formula 5000 Championship and was awarded South Africa's Springbok honors, his nation's highest sports commendation. Scheckter retired in 1980, at age thirty.

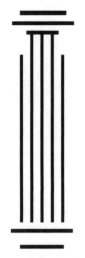 # BASEBALL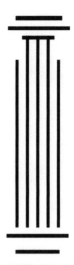

BARNEY DREYFUSS
United States
Born February 23, 1865, in Freiberg, Germany
Died February 1932

Barney Dreyfuss was owner of the National League Pittsburgh Pirates from 1900 to 1932, and creator of modern baseball's World Series. An innovator during professional baseball's tumultuous formative years, Dreyfuss built the first modern steel-frame triple-tier stadium, Forbes Field, in 1909.

In 1890, Dreyfuss obtained part ownership of the Louisville Colonels, then a Major League team in the American Association. In late 1899, he acquired the Pittsburgh Pirates team, bringing with him from Louisville such future Hall of Famers as Honus Wagner, Rube Waddell, and Fred Clarke. During his 32-year reign as President and General Manager of the Pirates, Pittsburgh finished in the first division 26 times, winning six pennants—1901, 1902, 1903, 1909, 1925, 1927—and the World Series in 1909 and 1925. During that time he led the successful fight to obtain a commissioner for baseball with jurisdiction over all Major League teams.

A baseball visionary who rose above the petty disputes rampant in the sport at the turn of the century, Dreyfuss arranged the first World Series in 1903, when the Boston Pilgrims, champions of the up-start American League, accepted his challenge to meet the National League Champion Pirates in an eight-game post-season tournament. The Pirates lost, but the World Series became a permanent fixture in baseball.

Dreyfuss was also a pioneer in professional football, as co-owner and manager of the Pittsburgh Athletic Club, winners of the pro-football championship in 1898—professional football's fourth organized season.

HENRY "HANK" GREENBERG
United States
Born January 1, 1911, in New York City
Died September 19, 1986

One of baseball's greatest right-handed hitters, Hank Greenberg starred as the Detroit Tigers' first baseman-outfielder, 1933–46 (in military service 1941–44), finishing his active career in 1947 with the Pittsburgh Pirates.

Greenberg was the American League's Most Valuable Player in 1935 and 1940. He won the American League home run Championship four times—in 1935, 1938, 1940 and 1946—hitting 31 career homers, including 11 grand slams. He held the Major League single season record of most games with two or more home runs in a game—11, in 1938; and that same year tied two Major League single season marks—(1) most home runs by a right-handed batter, 58 (only Roger Maris, Babe Ruth, and Jimmie Foxx hit as many or more); and, (2) hitting four homers on consecutive appearances in two games.

Greenberg had a lifetime batting average of .313, with 1,276 career runs-batted-in, including 183 in 1937, 170 in 1935, and 139 in 1934. Seven times he drove in move than 100 runs in a season. His statistics are all the more startling when compared to the number of games played in his career,

Hank Greenberg, the American League's Most Valuable Player in 1935 and 1940.

1,394—he played only 12 games in the 1936 season because of a broken wrist, was drafted into military service only 19 games into the 1941 season, and did not return to baseball until July of the 1945 season. Greenberg also played in four World Series for Detroit, batting .318, hitting five home runs and 22 RBIs in 23 games.

Already en route to becoming a baseball legend during his second big league season in 1934—he would finish the year with a .339 batting average, 139 RBIs, and lead the League in doubles—Greenberg became an indelible signature in both Jewish and baseball folklore. With Rosh Hashonah approaching and the Tigers moving closer to their first American League pennant in 25 years, fans, rabbis, and the media were caught up in a controversy concerning whether or not Greenberg should play in a game scheduled on Rosh Hashonah, the Jewish New Year.

After considerable soul-searching, Greenberg played on the holiday, hitting two home runs in a Detroit victory. However, there was also a game scheduled a week later on Yom Kippur—the holiest day of the Jewish year. Greenberg did not play that day, opting to spend the holy day in synagogue, and the Tigers lost. Nonetheless, Detroit won the pennant, and Greenberg won the respect of his peers, the fans of baseball, and the general public who followed his front-page story in the media. The popular American poet Edgar Guest was moved to write:

> Come Yom Kippur—holy fast day world-wide over to the Jew—
> And Hank Greenberg to his teaching and the old tradition true
> Spent the day among his people and he didn't come to play.
> Said Murphy to Mulrooney, "We shall lose the game today!
> We shall miss him in the infield and shall miss him at the bat,
> But he's true to his religion—and I honor him for that."

Greenberg was selected to four consecutive All Star teams, 1937–40. He was elected to the Baseball Hall of Fame in 1956.

SANFORD "SANDY" KOUFAX
United States
Born December 30, 1935, in Brooklyn, New York

The most dominant pitcher of his time, Sandy Koufax played for the Brooklyn and Los Angeles Dodgers from 1955 to 1966. He was the first pitcher in Major League baseball to hurl four no-hit games, including a perfect game in 1965.

Koufax won the Cy Young Award (baseball's highest pitching honor) three times in four years (1963, 1965, 1966), won the earned run average title five consecutive seasons (1962–66), won 25 or more games three times, had 11 shutouts in 1963, and 40 career shutouts. He was the Major League strikeout leader four times, including a record 382 strikeouts in 1965, 2,396 career strikeouts, and had three seasons with 300 or more strikeouts. In his final season, he was professional baseball's highest salaried player, and led his team to the World Series with a 27–9 record, and a 1.73 earned-run-average.

A severe arm injury caused his early retirement following the 1966 season. In 1972, Koufax became the youngest player ever elected to the Baseball Hall of Fame.

CHARLES "BUDDY" MYER
United States
Born March 16, 1904, in Ellisville, Mississippi
Died October 1974

Buddy Myer won the American League batting championship in 1935 with a .349 average. A Major League shortstop and second basemen, 1925–41, with the Washington Senators (mostly) and Boston Red Sox, he finished his career with a lifetime .303 batting average. He was with the Senators for 15 of his 17 seasons, spending 1927–28 with the Red Sox. Myer hit .300 or more nine times during his career, with his lowest full-season batting average .279. With the Red Sox in 1928, he won the American League base-stealing title

Sandy Koufax, the first Major League pitcher to throw four no-hit games.

with 30 thefts. The Senators re-acquired Myer for the 1929 season in a trade for five players, converting him from shortstop to the second-base position. In 1935, he set the American League doubleplay record for second baseman with 138 twin killings. That year proved to be his banner big league season, as Myer finished fourth in the Most Valuable Player balloting, behind winner Hank Greenberg.

Myer was elected to the All Star game twice, in 1935 and 1938. Myer's career stats include 2,131 hits in 1,923 games and, for a batter who generally hit at the top of the line-up, 850 rbi's.

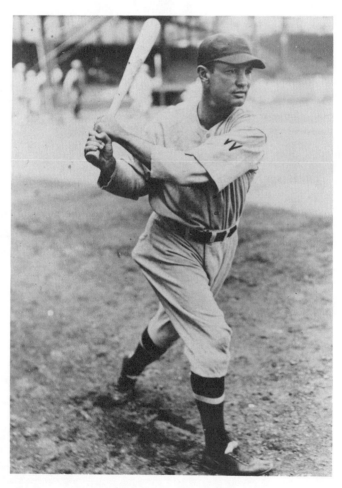

The Washington Senators' Buddy Myer in 1935, en route to a .349 average and the American League batting title.

LIPMAN "LIP" PIKE
United States
Born May 25, 1845, in New York City
Died October 1893

Accepting $20 a week to play third base for the Philadelphia Athletics in 1866, Lip Pike became baseball's first professional player. Other top players soon followed suit, and within three years, the first all-pro team was born in Cincinnati.

In 1871, the National Association—the first professional league—was founded, and Pike played and managed the N.A. Troy Haymakers, batting .351. His six-year National Association batting average was .321. His four-year National League average was .304.

Pike was also baseball's first home-run champion. Although the exact number of his round-trippers is not known, records show that he hit six homers in one game in July 1866. Primarily an outfielder, Pike played every position, and batted and threw left-handed. His career spanned 22 years, 1865–87, playing or playing/managing numerous teams in six different leagues. Among his teams were the Brooklyn Atlantics, Philadelphia Athletics, Lord Baltimores, Troy Haymakers, St. Louis Brown Stockings, Cincinnati Red Stockings, Hartford Nutmegs, and the original New York Mets.

Pike's athletic career was not confined to baseball. Known for his remarkable speed, he ran competitively—often running for cash purses in challenge races. He once raced and beat a famous trotting horse named "Clarence" in a 100-yard sprint (in 10 seconds flat), winning a $250 prize.

AL "FLIP" ROSEN
United States
Born March 1, 1925, in Spartanburg, South Carolina

A third-baseman playing with the American League Cleveland Indians, 1947–56, he was Major League baseball's first-ever unanimous selection as Most Valuable Player in 1953.

For five consecutive seasons, 1950–54, Rosen knocked in 100 or more runs each year. He led the American League in runs-batted-in in 1952 (105) and 1953 (145), and was home run champion twice: in 1950 (37 HRs) and in 1953 (43 HRs). With 1950 considered his rookie year, he was the first rookie to win the home run title. In 1953, he barely missed the coveted Triple Crown when his .336 batting average fell .0011 short of winning the batting title.

Rosen led the American League in total bases in 1952 and 1953, as well as slugging average in 1953. Four consecutive times he was elected to the Major League All Star Game (1952–55), clubbing two home runs and five RBIs in the 1954 contest. Persistent injuries forced Rosen's premature retirement following the 1956 season.

Al Rosen drove in 100 or more runs five consecutive seasons for the Cleveland Indians.

Dolph Schayes, who, on January 11, 1958, became the highest scorer in NBA history, with 11,770 points.

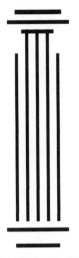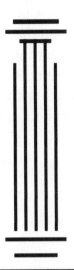

BASKETBALL

ARNOLD "RED" AUERBACH
United States
Born September 20, 1917, in Brooklyn, New York

Red Auerbach is the most successful professional basketball coach of all time. As head coach of the National Basketball Association's Boston Celtics from 1950 to 1966, his teams won nine World Championships—eight in succession, nine within ten years—and 11 division titles. The Auerbach-coached Celtics won 1,037 and lost 548.

Earlier, Auerbach coached the Basketball Association of America's (BAA) Washington Capitols, 1946–49, and the NBA's Tri-Cities, 1949–50. (The BAA and NBA merged in 1949.) His 1946–47 and 1948–49 Caps teams won division titles.

Becoming General Manager of the Celtics following his coaching career, Auerbach led the Boston team to NBA titles in 1968, 1969, 1974, 1980, and 1981. He was named NBA Executive of the Year in 1981.

Red has received practically every honor that can be bestowed on a professional basketball coach, including election to the Basketball Hall of Fame in 1968. In 1971, during the NBA's 25th Anniversary commemoration, he was named the "Silver Anniversary Coach," signifying the league's honor as best coach of its first quarter-century.

Auerbach's most colorful trademark was lighting up a long cigar on the team bench when he was certain his Celtics had a game "in the win column" —while the contest was still being played.

SENDA BERENSON
United States
Born March 19, 1868, in Vilna, Lithuania
Died 1952

In 1893, as the first Director of Physical Education at Smith College, Northampton, Massachusetts, Senda Berenson introduced women's basketball in the United States. In 1901, she published the first book of rules for women's basketball. Berenson held her position at Smith for 19 years (1892–1911) and served as chairperson of the United States Women's Basketball Committee from 1905 to 1917. In 1985, she was one of three women, the first females, inducted into the Basketball Hall of Fame.

LAWRENCE "LARRY" BROWN
United States
Born September 14, 1940, in Brooklyn, New York

A University of North Carolina basketball star, 1961–63, co-captain in 1963, Larry Brown won an Olympic gold medal in 1964 as a member of the champion United States basketball team.

Named to the 1963 All-Atlantic Coast Conference team and drafted by Baltimore of the National Basketball Association (NBA), Brown opted to play for Goodyear's (Akron, Ohio) AAU team, winning the Most Valuable Player Award in the 1964 AAU tournament. Brown played five seasons in the American Basketball Association (ABA)—three times an All-Star guard—with New Orleans, Oakland, Washington, Virginia, and Denver, averaging 11.3 points per game.

He turned to coaching in 1972, winning the ABA Championship with the Carolina Cougars in his rookie year. He won his second ABA crown with the Denver Nuggets, 1974–75, and was honored as ABA Coach of the Year. The Nuggets won their division title, 1975–76. Brown continued with the Denver franchise when it joined the NBA, 1976–77, winning two division titles in three seasons.

Brown followed with two successful years in the college coaching ranks at UCLA (University of California at Los Angeles). His Bruins finished second in the NCAA (National Collegiate Athletic Association) Tournament in 1980, and were ranked number 3 nationally in 1981. The following season, Brown was back coaching in the NBA, where he stayed for several years before returning to college basketball at the University of Kansas. His Jayhawks captured the coveted NCAA championship in 1988. Nevertheless, Brown returned to the pro game the very next season to helm the San Antonio Spurs. Inasmuch as Larry Brown continues to be an active coach, his record is incomplete.

Brown was a member of the 1961 USA Gold Medal Maccabiah Basketball Team.

ALEXANDER "SASCHA" GOMELSKY
Soviet Union
Born 1926 in Riga, Latvia

Sascha Gomelsky is the father of modern basketball in the Soviet Union. He is best recognized in the West as coach of the U.S.S.R. Olympic Basketball Team that won the controversial gold medal over the U.S.A. in the 1972 Munich Games. That still-debated victory resulted in the first-ever loss for the United States of an Olympic gold medal in basketball. Earlier, the

Gomelsky-coached Soviet basketball team had won a silver medal at the 1964 Tokyo Olympiad.

Gomelsky enjoyed numerous other successes as the U.S.S.R.'s National Coach. Although he has been relieved of his duties on several occasions when his National teams have failed to win major titles, he has always been recalled, and enjoys great popularity in and out of the Soviet Union. The success of Soviet basketball in the international arena is directly attributable to the coaching talents of this man.

Gomelsky began his coaching career in the Latvian Republic, later moving to Moscow to helm the prominent ZSKA team.

EDWARD "EDDIE" GOTTLIEB
United States
Born September 15, 1898, in Kiev, Russia
Died December 1979

Eddie Gottlieb was one of the founders of the National Basketball Association, and one of the innovative pioneers who held together pro basketball during its long and painful emerging decades.

Gottlieb coached the Philadelphia Warriors from 1947 to 1955, piloting them to the Basketball Association of America's first championship in 1947, and the NBA title in 1956. (The Basketball Association of America, 1947–49, merged into the NBA for the 1949–50 season.) Gottlieb purchased the Warriors in 1952 for $25,000, and saved professional basketball for the City of Philadelphia. He sold the franchise to San Francisco in 1962.

Prior to the establishment of the NBA, Gottlieb was associated with the legendary Philadelphia SPHAs (South Philadelphia Hebrew Association), first as a player in 1919, and subsequently as its coach. He led the SPHAs to 11 Eastern and American Basketball League championships, including the ABL titles in 1934, 1936, 1940, and 1945.

Many of pro basketball's existing rules are attributable to Gottlieb. From 1952, until his death in 1979, he was the official schedule-maker for the NBA. Gottlieb was inducted into the Basketball Hall of Fame in 1971.

NAT HOLMAN
United States
Born October 19, 1896, in New York City

Known as "Mr. Basketball," Nat Holman was one of the great players, coaches, and innovators of the sport. In 1950, American sportswriters named him to the First Team of the half-century, honoring him as the third greatest player from 1900 to 1950.

In 1919, at the age of 23, Holman became the youngest college coach in the United States, taking the basketball helm at City College of New York City (CCNY), a job he held until 1960 (except for three seasons in the 1950s).

As coach at CCNY, his teams boasted a remarkable 422–188 won-lost record. Holman's 1949–50 team was the first and last team to win the "grand slam" of American college basketball—championships of both the NCAA (National Collegiate Athletic Association) Tournament and the National Invitational Tournament in the same season.

While coaching at CCNY, the 5′11″ Holman played professional basketball on weekends with the New York Whirlwinds in 1920 and early 1921. He joined the legendary Original Celtics at the end of the 1921 season, and continued to play for them until 1929. Holman was regarded as the finest ball handler, playmaker, and set-shot artist of his day —a player with unmatched "court savvy" that helped lead the Celtics to an incredible 531–28 won-loss record.

It was with the Celtics that Holman devised the "center pivot" play, an offensive concept that revolutionized basketball. Every Celtic game was a virtual basketball clinic as college coaches flocked to watch Holman demonstrate his "cutting off the pivot" and executing the "give-and-go." In 1926, the Celtics joined the American Basketball League, but the team's lopsided winning ways continued. Having no reasonable competition to conquer, the Celtics disbanded in 1929.

Holman was a member of the group that in 1932 organized the American team for the first Maccabiah Games in Palestine. In 1949, under sponsorship of the U.S. State Department, Holman was the first American to coach in Israel, setting up clinics to develop the sport of basketball in the Holy Land. Under State Department auspices, he also conducted clinics in Japan, Korea, Taiwan, Mexico, Canada, and Turkey. In 1973, he began a term of four years as President of the United States Committee Sports for Israel, sponsors of the U.S. Maccabiah Games Team. Nat Holman was elected to the Basketball Hall of Fame in 1965.

WILLIAM "RED" HOLZMAN
United States
Born August 10, 1920, in New York City

At the time of his retirement, Red Holzman was the second-winningest coach in NBA history (Red Auerbach is number 1) with 696 victories in regular season play, mostly with the New York Knickerbockers. His Knicks won NBA championships in 1970 and 1973. He coached New York from December 1967 until his "retirement" in 1977. Red returned to the Knicks in November 1978, and continued through the 1981–82 season.

A City College of New York All-American in 1942, Holzman joined the professional Rochester Royals following World War II, and was an All-League player with the Club in 1946, when the Royals became one of the original franchise teams in the Basketball Association of America, predecessor of the NBA. Red was an All-Star member of the Royals' 1950–51 NBA Championship team, completing his active playing career in the 1953–54 season.

The following season, 1954–55, he began his NBA coaching career at Milwaukee (as player-coach), moving to St. Louis for the 1956–57 season.

HARRY LITWACK
United States
Born September 20, 1907, in Galicia, Austria

An institution in American college basketball, Harry Litwack was head coach of the Temple University Owls for 21 years, 1953–74, leading his team to 14 consecutive winning seasons. Perhaps the most important contribution Litwack made to the sport of basketball is the "zone defense," and innovation for which he is given credit. The "zone" changed the posture of the game, and made it necessary to develop totally new methods of coaching and playing.

An outstanding basketball player in his own right at Temple, 1927–29 (captain 1928–29), as well as star player and coach for several years of the Philadelphia SPHAs, Litwack's remarkable 21-year varsity coaching record at Temple was 373 wins/193 losses, including the 1969 National Invitational Championship. At his retirement in 1974, Litwack's record ranked fifth best among America's active college basketball coaches. He was elected to the Basketball Hall of Fame in 1975.

Litwack also coached the 1957 U.S.A. Maccabiah basketball team.

MAURICE PODOLOFF
United States
Born August 18, 1890, in Elizabethgrad, Russia
Died 1985

Maurice Podoloff was the first Commissioner of the National Basketball Association (1949–63), President of the Basketball Association of America (1946–49), President of the American Hockey League (1940–52), and President of the Canadian-American Hockey League (1936–40).

It was under Podoloff's leadership that the NBA developed the 24-second clock, the innovation credited as the foundation for the success of professional basketball in the United States.

In 1946, when the franchise owners of the American Hockey League organized the new Basketball Association of America, they elected Podoloff President of their new 11-team league. Three years later, he presided over the merger of the BAA and the new NBA. Podoloff was elected to the Basketball Hall of Fame in 1973.

MENDY RUDOLPH
United States
Born March 8, 1926, in Philadelphia, Pennsylvania
Died July 1979

Mendy Rudolph was a National Basketball Association referee for 25 years, 1953–78. He was the first (there have only been two) NBA floor official to work 2000 games, that historic event taking place in February, 1975. The quality of Rudolph's work is the standard by which today's basketball referees are measured.

ABE SAPERSTEIN
United States
Born July 4, 1902, in London, England
Died March 1966

Abe Saperstein was founder, owner, and coach of the Harlem Globetrotters Basketball Team. In 1927, following an unspectacular semi-pro baseball and professional basketball career (he stood 5'5"), Saperstein took over an all-black basketball team called the Savoy Big Five (named for Chicago's Savoy Ballroom), changed its name to the Harlem Globetrotters, and created a legend that is currently well into its second half-century.

The early Trotters were a traditional basketball five, sporting a 101–6 record their first year (1927), 145–13 in 1928, and 151–13 in 1929. Finding difficulty locating willing opponents, Saperstein conceived the idea of fancy, comedic, razzle-dazzle type of play, and soon the team became a must-see attraction on the basketball barnstorming circuit. It wasn't until 1940 that the Trotters started showing a profit, however, and through the many lean years Saperstein was not only its coach, chauffeur, and trainer, he was also the team's only substitute.

When the Globetrotters won the World Basketball Championship in 1940, they gave substance to Saperstein's long-ignored claim that, given the opportunity, they could play world-class basketball. In 1943–44, the Trotters won basketball's International Cup.

Over the years, the Globetrotters have developed into an international entertainment attraction, playing in more than 80 countries on five continents. They are undoubtedly the most famous sports organization in the world, with Saperstein labeled the "Barnum of Basketball," and his Trotters known as "America's number one goodwill ambassadors."

Saperstein was also a pioneer entrepreneur in America's Negro Baseball League, and was a key figure in opening the way for blacks into professional sports.

ADOLPH "DOLPH" SCHAYES
United States
Born May 19, 1928, in New York City

A New York University All-American in 1948, Dolph Schayes starred for the professional National Basketball Association Syracuse Nationals (later Philadelphia 76ers), 1948–64. His 1955 Nats won the NBA Championship. He was named to twelve consecutive NBA All Star Games, 1951–62. The League's Rookie of the Year in 1949, Schayes owned five NBA records by the time he retired as an active player: the most consecutive games played—764 (February 17, 1952, to December 27, 1961); the most minutes played—29,800; the most field goals—6,135; the most free throws made—6,979; and the most points—19,249.

He finished fourth all-time in rebounding, winning the rebound title in 1951 with 1,080 boards. On January 11, 1958, Schayes became the highest scorer in NBA history, reaching 11,770 points to surpass the great George Mikan. It was Wilt Chamberlain who eventually topped Schayes' scoring record. Regarded as the first true "power forward," Schayes had a career scoring average of 18.2 points per game.

He became player-coach of the 76ers in 1964, confining himself to coaching after that season. His Philadelphia team won the 1965–66 NBA Championship, and Schayes was named the League's Coach of the Year. From 1966 to 1970, he also served as supervisor of all NBA referees. He coached the NBA Buffalo Braves franchise, 1970–72.

In 1977, Schayes served as head coach of the U.S.A. Maccabiah Games basketball team. With the inspired play of his 6' 11" high-school-age son, Danny, the Americans won the gold medal.

BARNEY SEDRAN (SEDRANSKY)
United States
Born January 28, 1891, in New York City
Died January 1969

Elected to the Basketball Hall of Fame in 1962, Barney Sedran is considered one of the great professional basketball players of his era, 1912–25 —decades before the term "super star" was coined.

Standing only 5′ 4″, and 118 pounds, he and teammate Marty Friedman were known as the "Heavenly Twins." At a time of "barn-storming," short-term leagues, schedules that often called for nightly games and sometimes as many as three games a day, Sedran is said to have been the highest paid pro basketball star in the sport.

His New York Whirlwind team of 1919–21 is thought by many to have been the greatest professional basketball team in the first fifty years of the 20th century.

MAX ZASLOFSKY
United States
Born December 7, 1925, in Brooklyn, New York
Died October 1985

Max Zaslofsky was a professional basketball star between 1946 and 1956—with the Chicago Stags (1946–50), New York Knicks (1951–53), Baltimore and Milwaukee (1954), and Fort Wayne (1954–56). When he retired in 1956, Zaslofsky was the third highest scorer in NBA history with 7,990 points. He led the League in points in 1948 (21-point average), and was the NBA free-throw champion in 1950 with a 84.3 percentage.

Sylvia Wene Martin, who captured the BPAA Individual Match Game title in both 1955 and 1960.

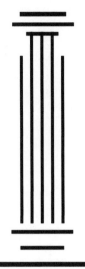 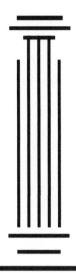

BOWLING

SYLVIA WENE MARTIN
United States
Born November 1930 in Philadelphia, Pennsylvania

One of the greatest women tenpin bowlers, Sylvia Wene Martin was best known as the lady bowler with the most 300 games (i.e. perfect games). A winner of numerous bowling crowns, she was the first woman to ever bowl three sanctioned 300 games, the first on March 28, 1951.

Her second perfecto came in the December 11, 1959, finals of the World Invitational Match Game Tournament. It was the first time a woman had scored 300 in match game competition. Just 28 days later, on January 8, 1960, she rolled her third 300 game—this time in the qualifying rounds of the Bowling Proprietors Association of America All-State Tournament, which she went on to win.

Martin twice captured the BPAA Individual Match Game title—1955 and 1960—and in both those years she was named Woman Bowler of the Year by the Bowling Writers Association of America. Other records include: all-time high League average of 206 (1952–55); 14 three-game "700" series (six in one year); member of the All-America teams five times—1955 and 1959–62. In 1965, Martin was elected to the Women's International Bowling Congress (WIBC) Hall of Fame.

MARK ROTH
United States
Born April 10, 1951, in Brooklyn, New York

Mark Roth is acknowledged by his peers as the "father of modern tenpin bowling." The hard-throwing, hard-cranking style that won him election to the Professional Bowlers Association Hall of Fame in April 1987 (the first year he was eligible) has brought about significant changes in the nature of alley bowling. From his first PBA title in 1975 (King Louie Open) to his last major tournament victory in 1987 (Greater Buffalo Open), Roth captured 34 PBA championships. He has received the PBA "Player of the Year" honor four times—1977–79 and 1984—and is the recipient of numerous other tenpin awards and titles. His 215-plus average over 8,000 games (dating back to 1976) is the best long-term pace in the history of the PBA.

Roth won the George Young Memorial High Average Award a record five times (three of four years between 1976–79, 1981, and 1988) and his 221.6 pace during the 1979 season is a PBA one-year-average record.

In 1984, Roth's career earnings elevated him to the PBA's "Millionaire's Club," joining ledgendary Earl Anthony as the association's second professional to reach the exclusive winners plateau. His most remarkable years were 1975 to 1979, when he captured 22 titles, including a record eight in 1978.

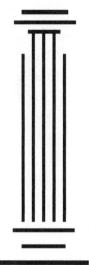
BOXING
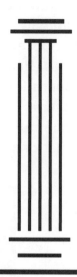

RAY ARCEL
United States
Born August 30, 1899, in Terre Haute, Indiana

Ray Arcel trained 20 World boxing champions—his first in 1923 and his most recent in 1982. In 1934, five of his fighters won World titles. In 1982, he became the first of only two trainers elected to the Boxing Hall of Fame. At one time, Arcel teamed with Whitey Bimstein to form the most successful training tandem in boxing.

Ray handled over two thousand fighters during his 70-year career in the ring, and none of them was ever seriously hurt. His World champions are: Frankie Genaro (Flyweight, 1923), Abe Goldstein (Bantamweight, 1924), Charlie Phil Rosenberg (Bantamweight, 1925), Jackie "Kid" Berg (Welterweight, 1930), Lou Brouillard (Middleweight, 1933), Teddy Yarosz (Middleweight, 1934), Barney Ross (Lightweight, 1933, and Welterweight, 1934), Sixto Escobar (Bantamweight, 1934), Bob Olin (Light-Heavyweight, 1934),

Jim Braddock (Heavyweight, 1934), Tony Marino (Bantamweight, 1936), Freddie Steele (Middleweight, 1937), Ceferino Garcia (Middleweight, 1939), Billy Soose (Middleweight, 1941), Tony Zale (Middleweight, 1946), Ezzard Charles (Heavyweight, 1950), Kid Gavilan (Welterweight, 1951), Alphonse "Peppermint" Fraser (Jr. Welterweight, 1972), Roberto Duran (Lightweight, 1972, and Welterweight, 1980), and Larry Holmes (Heavyweight, 1982).

Champions Rosenberg, Berg, and Ross have been elected to the International Jewish Sports Hall of Fame.

Ray Arcel (at right) raising the arm of World Middleweight Champion Tony Zale, June 10, 1948, following Zale's third-round KO of Rocky Graziano.

ABE ("The Little Hebrew") ATTELL

United States

Born February 22, 1884, in San Francisco, California
Died February 1970

Abe Attell was World Featherweight Champion, 1903–4 and 1906–12. The 5'4" / 122-pound teenager won his title four months short of his 18th birthday, defeating Johnny Reagan in 20 rounds. He lost the crown to Tony Sullivan one year later, but regained it in February 1906, with a decision over Jimmy Walsh.

Attell successfully defended his championship 21 times during the nine years he held the title. The complete fighter, Attell was both boxer and puncher, winning 23 of his first 29 fights by knockout. Attell claimed to have fought 365 bouts. But although his official record indicates less than half that number, he was known to have boxed as often as three times a week, frequently giving away as much as 30 pounds to an opponent. His official professional record: 171 bouts—124 wins (53 by KO), 19 losses, 24 draws, 2 no-decisions, 2 no-contests.

Attell was elected to the Boxing Hall of Fame in 1955.

SAMUEL BERGER

United States

Born December 25, 1884, in Chicago, Illinois
Died February 1925

Samuel Berger was the first Olympic Heavyweight Boxing Champion, winning his gold medal at the 1904 St. Louis Olympiad. (The St. Louis Games marked the first time boxing was included on the Olympic program.) A longtime leading amateur boxer representing the San Francisco Olympic Club, the 6'2"/200-pound heavyweight turned professional immediately after the Olympics, but fought only two years. His most notable pro bout was a six-round no-decision against Light-Heavyweight Champion "Philadelphia Jack" O'Brien in July 1906.

Sam Berger (left) en route to the first Olympic Heavyweight Boxing Championship at the 1904 Olympiad in St. Louis.

JOE CHOYNSKI
("Chrysanthemum Joe")
United States
Born November 8, 1868, in San Francisco, California
Died January 1943

Although he was never given a chance to fight for the World Heavyweight Championship, Joe Choynski nevertheless fought the great boxers of his time in non-title matches. Unfortunately for "Chrysanthemum Joe," who often gave away 30–70 pounds in a match, the Light-Heavyweight division wasn't created until 1903, a year before he retired.

In 1894, at 5' 10" and weighing less than 170 pounds, Choynski KO'd future heavyweight champion Bob Fitzsimmons in the fifth round of their non-title bout. Three years later, Joe fought heavyweight champion-to-be Jim Jeffries to a 20-round draw. In 1901, Choynski stopped the great Jack Johnson (before Johnson's heavyweight crown) in three rounds. He also battled young Jim Corbett five times, losing each non-title barn-burning bout.

When Fitzsimmons, Jeffries, Johnson, and Corbett were World

Champions, they refused to give Choynski a title bout. Both Fitzsimmons and Corbett were later to acknowledge that the hardest blows they ever took in the ring were delivered by Choynski. Said Corbett, about their June 1899 bout, in his autobiography, *The Roar of the Crowd* (1925): "[Choynski] was to be the very toughest battle I had ever fought or was to fight; one in which I was to receive more punishment than I have ever had in all my battles put together. . ." Jeffries, commenting on his draw with Joe, said, "In that fight, I received the hardest blow I ever took in my life."

Choynski retired in 1904, after 20 years in the ring. As testimony to his regard in the boxing world, he was elected to the Boxing Hall of Fame in 1960, long before most World Champions were to be so honored. His professional record: 77 bouts—50 wins (25 KOs), 14 losses, 6 draws, 6 no-decisions, and 1 no-contest.

ROBERT COHEN
France (Algeria)
Born November 15, 1930, in Bône, Algeria

Robert Cohen was World Bantamweight Champion from 1954 to 1956. Prior to his World titles he held the French and European Bantamweight crowns. His professional record: 43 bouts—36 wins (14 KOs), 4 losses, 3 draws.

*Robert Cohen, World Bantamweight Boxing Champion, 1954–56—one of two Jewish
Algerians to hold the title.*

JACKIE FIELDS (Jacob Finkelstein)
United States
Born February 9, 1908, in Chicago, Illinois
Died 1984

The World Welterweight Champion from 1929 to 1930 and from 1932 to 1933, Jackie Fields was only 16 years old in 1924 when he captured the Olympic Featherweight Championship—the youngest ever to win an Olympic boxing crown. Legendary fight manager Jack Kearns (in 1962) called Fields the "best all-around battler the United States has ever produced."

As an amateur, Fields won 51 of 54 bouts. His professional record: 87 fights—74 wins (30 KOs), 3 draws, 9 losses, 1 no-contest.

Jackie Fields in 1932 as World Welterweight Champion.

ALPHONSE HALIMI
France (Algeria)
Born January 18, 1932, in Constantine, Algeria

Alphonse Halimi was World Bantamweight Champion, 1957–59. He held the French Amateur Bantamweight title from 1953 to 1955, and won the All-Mediterranean title in 1955, turning professional after 189 amateur fights.

After losing his World title, Halimi regained the European Bantamweight crown in 1960. He lost that title again a year later, only to win it for the third time on June 26, 1962, in Tel Aviv, Israel. The bout marked the first-ever professional boxing match held in the State of Israel. Halimi's professional record: 50 bouts—41 wins, 8 losses, 1 draw.

LOUIS "KID" KAPLAN
United States
Born October 15, 1901, in Kiev, Russia
Died October 1970

World Featherweight Champion, 1925–26, Kid Kaplan defended his crown only three times before outgrowing the Featherweight division. After vacating his title, Kaplan was often referred to as the "Uncrowned Lightweight Champion," a compliment given him after top lightweight fighters of the era—such as Tony Canzoneri, Al Singer, and Al Mandell—refused to fight him and his punishing style. Kaplan's professional record: 150 bouts—108 wins (26 KOs), 13 draws, 17 losses, 12 no-contests.

BENNY LEONARD
(Benjamin Leiner)
United States
Born April 7, 1896, in New York City
Died April 1947

World Lightweight Champion from 1917 to 1925, Benny Leonard retired his crown undefeated. One of the greatest boxers and punchers in any weight to ever take the ring, Leonard lost his first professional fight and then went on to win 88 matches—68 by knockout.

In his first year as Champion, he defended his title 14 times, beginning just one week after winning it. Although Leonard retired from the ring a millionaire, he lost nearly everything in the stock market crash of 1929. After a seven-year layoff, he attempted an ill-fated comeback, retiring once again after losing to young Jimmy McLarnin in October 1932.

Commented veteran sports writer Dan Parker: "Leonard (as champion) moved with the grace of a ballet dancer and wore an air of arrogance that belonged to royalty." Said Hearst papers editor Arthur Brisbane of Leonard: "He has done more to conquer anti-Semitism than a thousand textbooks." In addition to the influence of his professional success, Leonard was an early supporter of the 1932 (the first) Maccabiah Games and the Games of 1935.

After several years in the U.S. Maritime Service during World War II, Leonard returned to boxing in 1943 as a referee. Four years later, he collapsed and died in the ring while refereeing a match in New York's St. Nicholas Arena. His professional record: 213 bouts—180 wins (69 KOs), 21 losses, 6 draws, 6 no-decisions. Leonard was elected to the Boxing Hall of Fame in 1955.

Benny Leonard held the World Lightweight title for nine years, retiring undefeated.

BATTLING LEVINSKY
(Barney Lebrowitz)
United States
Born June 10, 1891, in Philadelphia, Pennsylvania
Died February 1949

World Light-Heavyweight Champion from 1916 to 1920, Battling Levinsky began his boxing career under the name of Barney Williams, but got little attention until he took on a manager named "Dumb" Dan Morgan in 1913, who changed his name and his boxing fortunes.

True to his new name, Battling Levinsky fought 37 times in 1914—nine times during the month of January. In January of 1915, he began the year with three ten-round bouts on New Year's Day—one each in Brooklyn, Waterbury (Connecticut), and New York City. After two title-match losses to Light-Heavyweight Champion Jack Dillon (April 1914 and April 1916), Levinsky wrested the crown from Dillon on October 24, 1916. 59 bouts later, almost four years to the day, he lost his championship to France's Georges Carpentier.

In an era when boxing titles changed hands only because of a knockout—non-KO championship fights were labeled "no-decision"— Levinsky fought all comers, including Heavyweight champions-to-be Gene Tunney and Jack Dempsey (losing both matches). Levinsky loved to fight, although his claim to having fought as many as 500 bouts is impossible to substantiate.

His official professional record: 287 bouts—192 wins (34 KOs), 52 losses, 34 draws, 9 no-decisions. Levinsky was elected to the Boxing Hall of Fame in 1966.

TED "KID" LEWIS
(Gershon Mendeloff)
Great Britain
Born October 24, 1894, in London, England
Died October 1970

Kid Lewis was World Welterweight Champion from 1915 to 1916 and again from 1917 to 1919. Nicknamed the "Aldgate Sphinx," he fought in six divisions during his 20-year career.

Lewis became England's youngest boxing champion in October 1913, when at age 17 he won the British Featherweight title. Just a few months later, in February 1914, he captured the European Featherweight crown.

When Lewis won a 12-round decision over Jack Britton (America's leading welterweight) in Boston on August 31, 1915, he became the first Brit to win a World title in the United States. The two were to fight 20 times from 1915 to 1921, with Lewis losing the title to Britton in 1916, regaining it the following year, and losing it for the final time in March, 1919.

Lewis relinquished his claim to the British Empire and European Welterweight titles in late 1920; and in early 1921 won both the British and European Middleweight championships. In 1922, although he lost, Lewis fought Georges Carpentier (the reigning World Light-Heavyweight Champion) for the European Heavyweight championship. Lewis lost the last of his European boxing crowns in November 1924.

The sport of boxing has long been indebted to Lewis and his dentist, Jack Marks, albeit in virtual anonymity. In 1913, Kid Lewis was the first boxer to use a mouthpiece, a piece of special equipment that was designed for him by Marks, an ex-fighter. The mouthpiece soon became—and continues to be—standard equipment in the sport of boxing.

Lewis's professional record: 283 bouts—215 wins (71 KOs), 44 losses, 24 draws. Lewis was elected to the Boxing Hall of Fame in 1964.

AL McCOY
(Al Rudolph)
United States
Born October 23, 1894, in Rosenhayn, New Jersey
Died August 1966

At the age of 18, Al McCoy won the World Middleweight Championship, and he held the title from 1914 to 1917. He was the first southpaw (left-hander) ever to win a World Championship. His professional record: 157 bouts—75 wins (26 KOs), 40 losses, 24 draws, 18 no-decisions.

DANIEL MENDOZA
Great Britain
Born July 5, 1764, in London, England
Died September 1836

Daniel Mendoza was the first Jewish prizefighter to become a champion. Though he stood only 5'7", and weighed just 160 pounds, Mendoza was England's 16th Heavyweight Champion (World Champion) from 1794 to 1795. Always proud of his heritage, he billed himself as "Mendoza the Jew."

He is the father of scientific boxing. At a time when the sport of boxing consisted primarily of barehanded slugging, Mendoza introduced a system of defense. He developed the guard, the straight left, and made use of side-stepping tactics. This new strategy, the "Mendoza School" (also referred to as the "Jewish School"), was criticized in some circles as cowardly. But it permitted Mendoza to fully capitalize on his small stature, speed, and punching power. A victory in his first professional fight in 1790 won him the patronage of the Prince of Wales, the first boxer to earn this honor.

Mendoza's acceptance by British royalty (he was the first Jew ever to speak to England's King George III) helped elevate the position of the Jew in English society and to stem a vicious tide of anti-Semitism that many

Englishmen read into Shakespeare's characterization of Shylock in his play *The Merchant of Venice.*

Mendoza became such a popular figure in England that songs were written about him, his name appeared in scripts of numerous plays, his personal appearances would fill theaters, portraits of him and his fights were popular subjects for artists, and commemorative medals were struck in his honor.

Daniel Mendoza was one of the inaugural group chosen in 1954 for the Boxing Hall of Fame.

SAMUEL MOSBERG
United States
Born June 14, 1896, in New York City
Died August 1967

Samuel Mosberg won the Olympic Lightweight (135-pound) Championship at the 1920 Games in Antwerp, Belgium. En route to his gold medal, Mosberg scored what historians recall as the quickest knockout in Olympic boxing history, finishing an opponent in a matter of seconds.

In a career that began in 1912, Mosberg fought 250 amateur fights prior to turning pro after the Olympics. He retired in 1923 with 57 professional fights under his belt, enjoying limited success. Said Spike Webb, the perennial U.S.A. Olympic boxing coach during the first half of the 20th century: "Sammy Mosberg is the greatest Olympic champion I ever coached." Webb's Olympic protegés included: gold medalists Jackie Fields, Fidel LaBarba, and Frankie Genaro—all of whom went on to become World professional champions.

Mosberg coached the United States boxing team at the 1953 Maccabiah Games.

VICTOR "YOUNG" PEREZ
Tunisia
Born October 18, 1911, in Tunis
Died February 1943

Victor Perez was the World Flyweight Champion from 1931 to 1932. He captured the French Flyweight title in Paris in June 1931, and won the International Boxing Union's version of the World Flyweight crown in October of the same year, with a second-round knockout of American champion Frankie Genaro.

After losing his title one year later, Perez moved up to the Bantamweight class, but lost a championship bout decision to Al Brown in February 1934. He continued to box until December, 1938.

Four year later, Perez died in the Auschwitz concentration camp.

His official professional record: 133 bouts—92 wins (28 KOs), 26 losses, 15 draws.

CHARLEY PHIL ROSENBERG
(Charles Green)
United States
Born August 15, 1902, in New York City
Died March 1976

World Bantamweight Champion from 1925 to 1927, Charley Rosenberg captured his title on March 20, 1925, in New York City, beating Eddie Martin in a 15-round decision. In order to make weight for the fight, Rosenberg had to lose 39 pounds in ten weeks.

He remained champion until February 4, 1927, when he won a 15-round title defense against Bushy Graham, but was forced to relinquish his crown when he could not make the division's legal weight. Rosenberg fought only two more bouts (won both) before deciding to retire, including a victory over former Featherweight Champion Johnny Dundee. His professional record: 65 bouts—33 wins (7 KOs), 8 draws, 17 losses, 7 no-decisions.

Charley Phil Rosenberg defeats Eddie "Cannonball" Martin, March 20, 1925, at Madison Square Garden, to win the World Bantamweight Championship.

MAXIE "SLAPSIE MAXIE" ROSENBLOOM
United States
Born September 6, 1904, in Leonard's Bridge, Connecticut
Died March 1976

World Light-Heavyweight Boxing Champion from 1930 to 1934, Maxie Rosenbloom was the busiest title holder in ring history, fighting 106 times during his four-and-a-half-year reign—the equivalent of fighting one bout every 15 days!

Newspaperman Damon Runyon, writing about Rosenbloom's colorful persona and his unique open glove style of boxing, dubbed him "Slapsie Maxie," a nickname that stuck with him throughout his career. Rosenbloom's sharp wit and broken syntax brought him new success with motion picture audiences following his ring retirement. He appeared in nearly 100 films during his entertainment career. He was elected to the Boxing Hall of Fame in 1972. Rosenbloom's professional record: 299 bouts—223 wins (19 KOs), 42 losses, 32 draws, 2 no-contests.

BARNEY ROSS
(Barnet David Rosofsky)
United States
Born December 23, 1909, in New York City
Died January 1967

Barney Ross was World Lightweight and Junior Welterweight Champion from 1933 to 1935, and World Welterweight Champion, 1934 and 1935–38. He was the first professional boxer to hold the Lightweight and Welterweight crowns simultaneously.

Ross beat Tony Canzoneri for the World Lightweight and World Junior Welterweight titles on June 23, 1933. On May 28, 1934, he beat Jimmy McLarnin for the World Welterweight crown, but lost it back to McLarnin on

September 17th of the same year. Ross relinquished his World Lightweight crown in April of 1935, and barely a month later, regained his World Welterweight title from McLarnin. He then relinquished his Junior Welter-weight title. Ross held on to his Welterweight crown until May 31, 1938, when he lost it to Henry Armstrong.

Including his extraordinary amateur boxing career, Ross fought 329 bouts, 81 of them as a pro. His professional record: 74 wins (22 knockouts), 4 losses (all by decision), 3 draws. Ross was elected to the Boxing Hall of Fame in 1956.

LEW TENDLER
United States
Born September 28, 1898, in Philadelphia, Pennsylvania
Died November 1970

Lew Tendler is called "the greatest southpaw [left-hander] in ring history," by *Ring* magazine's editor-publisher Nat Fleischer. In 1961, he became the sixteenth prizefighter elected to the Boxing Hall of Fame. Yet, as great a fighter as he was, Tendler never won a ring championship.

A brilliant lightweight and welterweight, Tendler made just one career "mistake": fighting in the same era as legendary Benny Leonard. Tendler would meet champion Leonard in two classic and wildly heralded matches, losing the first bruising battle on a "no decision." Although the younger Tendler had soundly thrashed Leonard throughout the 12-round bout, the State of New Jersey—site of the July 27, 1922, match—had a "no decision" law, in effect meaning that a champion could only lose his title by a knockout. On July 24, 1923, almost a year-to-the-day later, a New York City crowd of 58,519 paid $452,648—at the time the largest gate ever for the lightweight division—to see the pair clash again for the title. This time Leonard prevailed in a 15-round decision—decisions being legal in the State of New York. Eleven months later, Tendler moved up a weight class and battled Mickey Walker for the World Welterweight crown, losing a ten-round decision. Tendler's professional record: 167 bouts—59 wins (37 KOs), 2 draws, 11 losses, 94 no-decisions, 1 no-contest.

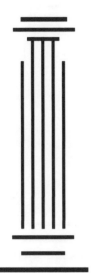
CANOEING
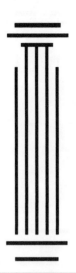

LEON ROTTMAN
Romania
Born July 22, 1934, in Bucharest

Leon Rottman won two gold medals at the 1956 Melbourne Olympic Games, one in the 1,000-meter Canadian Singles (5:05.3), and another in the 10,000-meter Canadian Singles (56:41.0). He also won a bronze medal at the 1960 Olympiad in Rome in the 1,000-meter Canadian Singles (4:35.87).

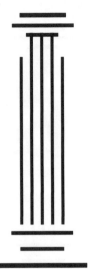
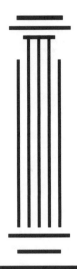

CRICKET

ARON "ALI" BACHER
South Africa
Born May 24, 1942, in Johannesburg

One of the greatest cricketeers in South African history, Ali Bacher played in 12 "test" matches for his country, captaining his teams in four of those matches. Making his first class debut in 1959 at age 17, he made a total of 120 first class appearances during his career, scoring 7,894 runs, averaging 39.07 per match. Bacher scored 18 centuries, and made 110 catches. He captained the Balfour Park Cricket Team in 1962, and captained Transvaal the following year.

Bacher's highest single match score came against Australia in 1966, when he rang up 235 runs for his Transvaal side in the first ever victory for a S.A. team against an Australian team in South Africa. Bacher cut short his playing career in 1974, at only 31 years old, when South Africa was banned from international competition. In 1972, he was awarded South Africa's Sports Merit Award, that country's highest athletics honor.

Jody Scheckter

Barney Dreyfuss

Henry "Hank" Greenberg

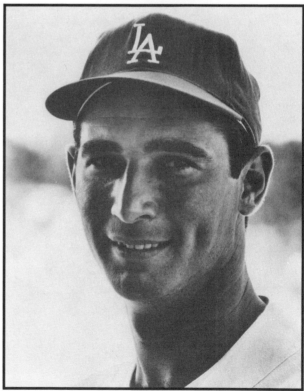

Sanford "Sandy" Koufax

Charles "Buddy" Myer

Lipman "Lip" Pike

Al "Flip" Rosen

Arnold "Red" Auerbach

Basketball

Senda Berenson

Lawrence "Larry" Brown

Alexander "Sascha" Gomelsky

Edward "Eddie" Gottlieb

Nat Holman

William "Red" Holzman

Harry Litwack

Maurice Podoloff

Basketball

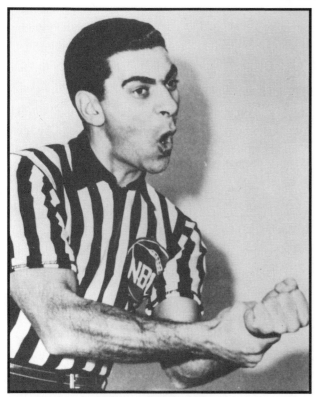

Mendy Rudolph

Abe Saperstein

Adolph "Dolph" Schayes

Barney Sedran

73

Basketball, Bowling, Boxing

Max Zaslofksy

Sylvia Wene Martin

Mark Roth

Ray Arcel

Abe Atell

Samuel Berger

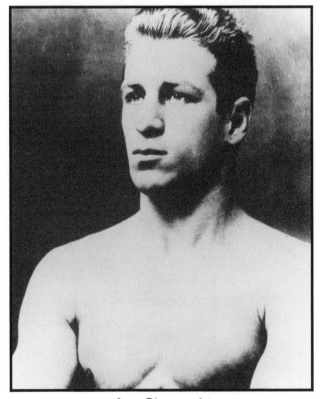

Joe Choynski

Robert Cohen

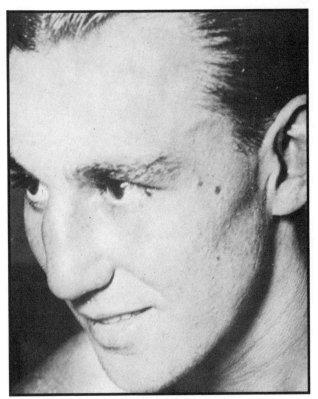

Jackie Fields

Alphonse Halimi

Louis "Kid" Kaplan

Benny Leonard

Boxing

Battling Levinsky

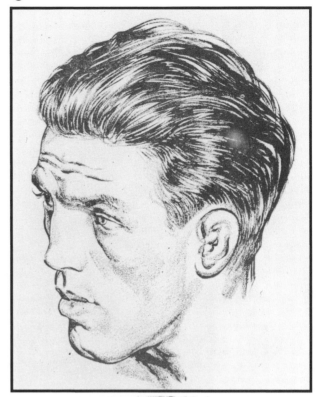

Ted "Kid" Lewis

Al McCoy

Daniel Mendoza

Samuel Mosberg

Victor "Young" Perez

Charley Phil Rosenberg

Maxie Rosenbloom

Barney Ross

Lew Tendler

Leon Rottman

Aron "Ali" Bacher

Fencing

Jeno Fuchs

Janos Garay

Oszkar Gerde

Allan Jay

Fencing

Endre Kabos

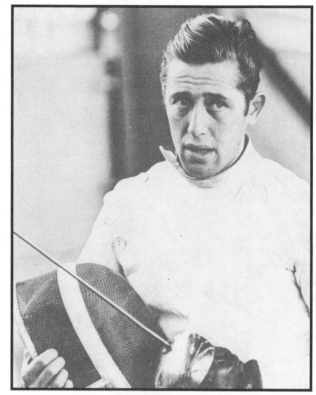

Grigori Kriss

Alexandre Lippmann

Mark Midler

Fencing

Ivan Osiier

Attila Petschauer

Mark Rakita

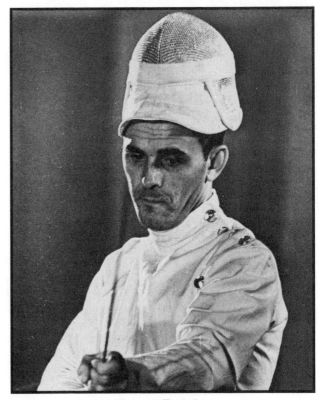

Yakov Rylsky

Alain Calmat

Lily Kronberger

Louis Rubenstein

Joseph Alexander

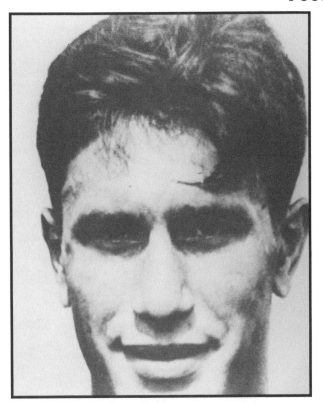

Benny Friedman

Sid Gillman

Marshall Goldberg

Sid Luckman

Ron Mix

Harry Newman

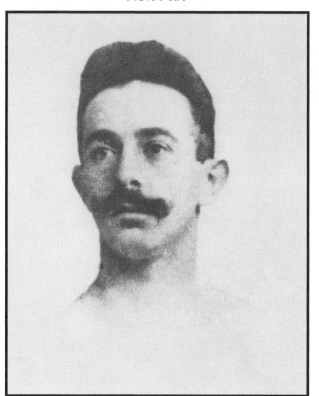

Alfred Flatow

Gustav Felix Flatow

Gymnastics

Mitch Gaylord

Maria Gorokhovskaya

Abie Grossfeld

George Gulack

Agnes Keleti

Vic Hershkowitz

Jimmy Jacobs

Cecil "Cece" Hart

Walter Blum

Hirsch Jacobs

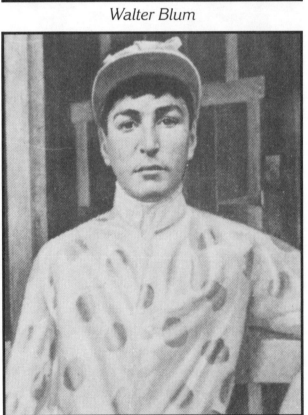

Walter Miller

Arthur Baar

Bela Guttmann

Hakoah Vienna Club

Gyula Mandel

Hugo Meisl

Irving Jaffee

Arthur Abraham Gold

Sir Ludwig Guttmann

Ferenc Mezoe

Zvi Nishri

Mel Allen

Charlotte Epstein

Alfred Hajos-Guttmann

Swimming

Otto Herschmann

Paul Neumann

Marilyn Ramenofsky

Mark Spitz

Eva Szekely

Angelica Adelstein-Rozeanu

Viktor Barna

Richard Bergmann

Table Tennis, Tennis

Ivor Goldsmid Montagu

Miklos Szabados

Angela Buxton

Herb Flam

Dick Savitt

Harold Abrahams

Lillian Copeland

Lilli Henoch

Track and Field

Maria Itkina

Elias Katz

Irena Kirszenstein-Szewinska

Abel Kiviat

Fania Melnik

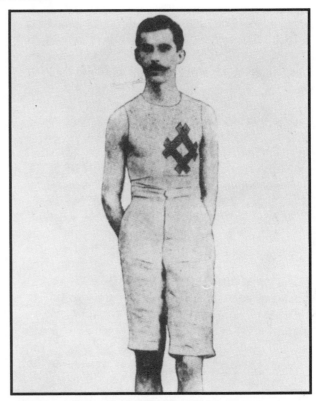

Laurence E. "Lon" Myers

Myer Prinstein

Fanny "Bobbie" Rosenfeld

György Brody

Miklos Sarkany

Isaac Berger

Edward Lawrence Levy

Grigori Novak

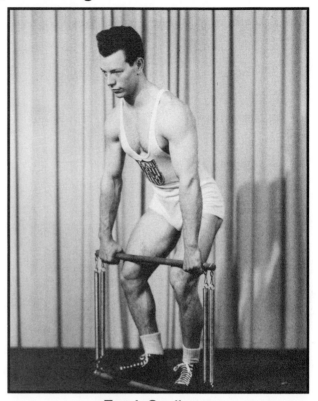

Frank Spellman

Boris Mendelovitch Gurevich

Boris Michail Gurevitch

Richard Weisz

Henry Wittenberg

Zefania Carmel and Lydia Lazarov

Walentin Mankin

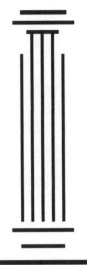 # FENCING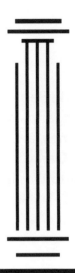

JENO FUCHS
Hungary
Born October 29, 1882, in Budapest
Died 1954

Jeno Fuchs was the winner of four Olympic gold medals. He won gold medal honors in Individual and Team Sabre at the 1908 London Olympic Games, and, four years later, posted repeat victories in the same events at the 1912 Games in Stockholm. Fuchs was undefeated at the 1912 Olympiad en route to his gold medals.

JANOS GARAY

Hungary

Born 1889 in Hungary
Date of death unknown

World Sabre Champion in 1925, Janos Garay won three Olympic medals for Hungary—silver in Team Sabre and bronze in Individual Sabre at the 1924 Games, and a gold medal in Team Sabre at the 1928 Olympics.

Garay is believed to have perished in a Nazi concentration camp during World War II.

OSZKAR GERDE

Hungary

Born July 8, 1883, in Budapest
Died October 1944

Oszkar Gerde won gold medals in Team Sabre at both the 1908 (London) and 1912 (Stockholm) Olympic Games. Little is known about Gerde outside his exceptional Olympic performances.

A medical doctor, Dr. Gerde perished in the concentration camp of Mauthausen, Austria.

ALLAN JAY

Great Britain

Born June 30, 1931, in London, England

World Foil Champion in 1959, Allan Jay won silver medals at the 1960 Rome Olympic Games in both Individual and Team Epee. In 1956, Jay finished fourth in the Foil event at the Olympic Games.

At the 1950 and 1953 Maccabiah Games in Israel, Jay won six gold medals in both Foil and Epee events.

The 1932 Hungarian gold medal Olympic fencing team: Atilla Petschauer (second from left) and Endre Kabos (fourth from left).

ENDRE KABOS
Hungary
Born November 5, 1906, in Budapest
Died November 1944

Endre Kabos was World Sabre Champion in 1933 and 1934. He won four Olympic medals for Hungary—gold in Team Sabre and bronze in Individual Sabre—at the 1932 games in Los Angeles; and gold medals in both Individual and Team Sabre at the 1936 Munich Olympics.

Kabos was killed in a World War II air raid in Budapest.

GRIGORI KRISS
Soviet Union
Born December 24, 1940, in Kiev, Ukraine

Grigori Kriss won four fencing medals for the Soviet Union over three Olympiads. He won his first gold in Individual Epee at the 1964 Tokyo Olympic Games. In 1968, he won silvers, each, in the Individual Epee and Team Epee events; and in 1972, he captured a bronze medal in Team Epee.

ALEXANDRE LIPPMANN
France
Born 1880
Date of death unknown

In three Olympiads, Alexandre Lippmann won five medals, including two golds. At the 1908 London Games, he won a gold medal in Team Epee and a silver in Individual Epee. (There were no Olympic Games in 1916.) At the Antwerp Games of 1920, Lippmann won a silver medal in Individual Epee and a bronze in Team Epee. In Paris in 1924, he won a gold medal in Team Epee, as his French team won another Olympic Championship.

MARK MIDLER
Soviet Union
Born September 24, 1931, in Moscow, Russia

A winner of two Olympic gold medals, Mark Midler also captured World Championship titles in the Foil event for four consecutive years, 1959 through 1962.

Midler became a member of the Soviet National team in 1954, and was named captain of the Russian fencers for the 1960 Olympic Games in Rome. He won his first gold medal in Team Foil at the Rome Olympiad, and repeated four years later in Tokyo—again as captain—as the Soviet fencers won their second consecutive Olympic Team Foil Championship.

ARMAND MOUYAL
France
Born October 16, 1925, in Paris

Mouyal was World Epee Champion in 1957. In 1956, he won an Olympic bronze medal in Team Epee at the Melbourne Games. (The author has been unable to secure a photograph or other likeness of Mouyal.)

IVAN OSIIER
Denmark
Born December 16, 1888
Died September 1965

One of few recipients of the Olympic Diploma of Merit, Ivan Osiier represented his country in seven Olympic Games between 1908 and 1948, missing only the 1936 Games, when he refused to participate in Berlin as a protest against the Nazis. He has participated in more Olympiads than any other athlete.

Osiier was a few months shy of age 60 when he won his first and only Olympic medal, a silver in Individual Epee, at the London Games of 1948—40 years *after* his Olympic debut (also in London). Dr. Osiier won a total of 25 Danish National Championships in all three weapons: foil, epee, sabre. He was also Scandinavian Foil Champion in 1920, 1921, 1923, 1927, 1929, and 1931, Epee Champion in 1920, and Sabre Champion in 1921, 1923, 1927, 1929, 1931, and 1933.

Olympiad medalist Ivan Osiier was also winner of 38 Danish and Scandinavian fencing medals.

ATTILA PETSCHAUER
Hungary
Born December 14, 1904, in Budapest
Died January 1943

Attila Petschauer won an Olympic gold medal in Team Sabre and a silver in Individual Sabre at the 1928 Amsterdam Games. Four year later, he won a gold medal in Team Sabre at the 1932 Los Angeles Olympiad.

In the Amsterdam Olympics, Petschauer actually finished in a tie with countryman Odon Tersztyanszky in Individual Sabre, but lost a fence-off for the gold medal.

Petschauer died in a Nazi labor camp in the Ukraine.

MARK RAKITA
Soviet Union
Born July 22, 1938, in Moscow, Russia

Sabre specialist Mark Rakita won Team event gold medals at the 1964 and 1968 Olympic Games, and a silver medal in the Individual Sabre event at the 1968 Games. He was considered one of the best of the first generation of outstanding Jewish fencers in the Soviet Union.

YAKOV RYLSKY
Soviet Union
Born October 25, 1928, in East Kazakhstan, Oblast

Yakov Rylsky won the World Sabre Championship in 1958, 1961, and 1963. In 1963 he captured the Dantzer Cup and, in 1964, won an Olympic gold medal in Team Sabre at the Tokyo Games. At his first Olympic competition, in Melbourne in 1956, Rylsky was a bronze medalist in Team Sabre.

A pioneer in the sport of fencing in the Soviet Union, Rylsky joined the Russian National Team in 1954, and is a Merited Master of Sports in the U.S.S.R. (the highest honor given to Soviet athletes).

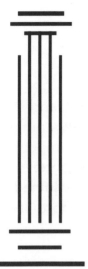

FIGURE
SKATING

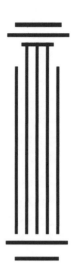

ALAIN CALMAT (Calmanovich)
France
Born August 31, 1940, in Paris

Alain Calmat won the World Figure Skating Championship in 1965. A silver medalist at the 1964 Winter Olympic Games, he also captured silver medals in the World Championships of 1963 and 1964. In 1962, 1963, and 1966, Calmat held the European Figure Skating titles.

At the 1968 Winter Games in Grenoble, Calmat was selected to carry the torch and light the Olympic flame—the first and only Jew to ever be so honored.

LILY KRONBERGER
Hungary
Born 1887
Date of death unknown

Kronberger reigned as World Figure Skating Champion from 1908 to 1911. Earlier, she finished third in the first official World Championships in 1906, and repeated her third-place ranking at the 1907 World Championships.

In winning her final World title in 1911, Kronberger was the first skater to attempt an entire free skating program with musical accompaniment.

LOUIS RUBENSTEIN
Canada
Born September 23, 1861, in Montreal, Quebec
Died January 1931

In 1890, Louis Rubenstein won first place in the first (unofficial) World Figure Skating Championships. The Championships were held in St. Petersburg (now Leningrad), Russia, where organizers tried first to prevent the Jewish skater from participating, and later tried to deny his victory.

He was North America's first famous figure skater, winning Canadian championships, 1883–89, the North American crown in 1885, and United States titles in 1888, 1889, and 1891.

Rubenstein was a career sportsman. After retiring from active skating, he held the presidency of various Canadian organizations involved with tenpin bowling, curling, bicycling, tobogganing, lifesaving, and skating. He is called "the father of Bowling in Canada."

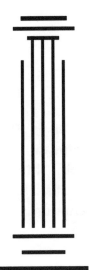 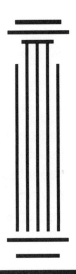

FOOTBALL

JOSEPH ALEXANDER
United States
Born April 1, 1898, in Syracuse, New York
Died 1975

Joseph Alexander was a three-time All-America lineman for Syracuse University, at guard in 1917 and 1918, and at center in 1919. Alexander's roving style was akin to the modern line-backer—unique in the early days of college football. From his line position, he was the team's offensive signal caller.

He played professional football with an assortment of teams, including the Rochester Jeffersons, Philadelphia Quakers, Frankford Yellow Jackets, Rochester Kodaks, Milwaukee Badgers, and, finally, the New York Giants, 1925–1927.

When the Giants were granted a National Football League franchise in 1925, Alexander was the first player signed by the team. He was named to the NFL All-Star team that year. A practicing medical doctor since his college

Joe Alexander

graduation in 1921, Alexander was also one of the few Giants to receive a yearly playing salary.

He took over as the Giants' head coach in 1926, but relinquished the job in his final year with the team. In 1937, the *New York World Telegram* named Alexander to its All-Time All-America Team at guard. Football expert George Trevor selected him as the greatest collegiate guard of the 1919–29 decade.

BENNY FRIEDMAN
United States
Born March 18, 1905, in Cleveland, Ohio
Died November 1982

As quarterback and halfback of the University of Michigan Wolverines, Benny Friedman was football's first great passer. He was selected first team All-America in 1925 and 1926. Friedman was the consummate "triple threat" man—passing, running, and kicking—moving easily from the college gridiron to professional football stardom.

He was All-Pro from 1927 to 1931, playing seven professional seasons beginning with the Cleveland Bulldogs in his rookie year. In 1928, Friedman starred for the Detroit Wolverines, then the New York Giants, 1929–31. The Giants purchased the entire Detroit team in order to acquire Friedman's contract, and the $10,000 they paid him made Benny the highest-paid player in the pro ranks. He finished his playing career with the Brooklyn Dodgers (football team), 1932–34.

In 1934, Friedman became head coach at City College of New York, a job he held until joining the U.S. Navy in 1941. From 1949 to 1963, he served as head football coach and athletic director at Brandeis University, Waltham, Massachusetts.

Friedman's multiple talents had a lasting effect on the evolution of football from a straight-forward running game to the modern pass-and-run game —not the least of which was the slenderizing of the football itself, to take better advantage of the forward pass. He was one of the first to be elected to the College Football Hall of Fame.

Benny Friedman, the consummate "triple threat" (passing, running, kicking), was one of the first players to be elected to the College Football Hall of Fame.

SID GILLMAN
United States
Born October 26, 1911, in Minneapolis, Minnesota

One of football's great innovators, Sid Gillman served as head coach of American professional football's Los Angeles Rams, 1955–59, and Los Angeles/San Diego Chargers, 1960–71.

Before he made his name as a professional coach, Gillman, an All-America end for Ohio State University in 1932 and 1933, served as either coach or head coach for 21 years at such colleges as Ohio State, Dennison (Ohio), Miami of Ohio, West Point, and Cincinnati. His college teams won 79, lost 18, and tied 2.

As head coach of the National Football League (NFL) Rams, Gillman won one Division title; and with the American Football League (AFL) Chargers, he captured five Division crowns as well as the 1963 AFL Championship. Gillman was the first head coach to win Divisional titles in both the NFL and AFL. Bad health forced his premature retirement in 1971.

The venerable Sid (also the Chargers general manager) is credited with the idea for the Super Bowl (the AFL versus the NFL), the use of game and practice films as an integral aspect of coaching, and he was the first to put the names of players on their jerseys. On the field, Gillman was a strong advocate and brilliant strategist of the wide-open forward pass offense, and is credited with being one of the developers of the "two-platoon system."

Some of Gillman's coaching protegés were: Al Davis, Chuck Noll, Bum Phillips, Dan Henning, Ara Parseghian, and Paul Dietzel. Many credit the success of the "upstart" American Football League to Gillman's skillful organizational techniques.

With improved health, Sid joined the Houston Oilers in 1973 as their general manager. Halfway through the season, he fired the head coach, took over the job, and led the Oilers on and off the field through 1974—after which he was fired. Nevertheless, he was named NFL Coach of the Year in 1974.

After health, again, forced him into retirement, Gillman resurfaced in 1977 as the Chicago Bears offensive coordinator. That year, the Bears made the League playoffs for the first time in 14 seasons. Sid moved to the

Philadelphia Eagles in 1979, but following heart by-pass surgery, his duties were narrowed to quarterback development.

Sid Gillman was elected to the Pro Football Hall of Fame in 1983.

MARSHALL "BIGGIE" GOLDBERG
United States
Born October 24, 1917, in Elkins, West Virginia

Marshall "Biggie" Goldberg (number 42) heading for a TD in 1938 at Pitt Stadium.

Marshall Goldberg was a two-time University of Pittsburgh All-America, in 1937 and 1938, and four-time National Football League (NFL) All-Pro.

A West Virginia high school legend, captaining his Elkins High

School football, basketball, and track teams in 1935, he was elected All-State in each sport.

Goldberg's 1936 Pitt football team won the Rose Bowl, and the 1937 eleven earned the National Collegiate Championship. In 29 varsity college games with the Pittsburgh Panthers, Goldberg, playing halfback and fullback, gained 2,231 yards and scored 18 touchdowns.

Playing on the woeful Chicago Cardinal NFL teams from 1939 through the early 1940s, Goldberg was named All-Pro in 1941, spending 1944–45 in military service. In an era when football players played both offense *and* defense, Goldberg was named All-Pro Defensive Back three consecutive years: 1946, 1947, and 1948. His Cardinals won the NFL Championship in 1947, and captured the Division title in 1948.

Sports Illustrated named Goldberg to the 1930s "College Football Team of the Decade." He is a member of the National Football Foundation Hall of Fame, and the Halls of Fame of West Virginia, the City of Pittsburgh, and Pop Warner Football.

SIDNEY "SID" LUCKMAN
United States
Born November 21, 1916, in Brooklyn, New York

An outstanding college football running and passing tailback at Columbia University, 1936–38, and selected All-America in 1937 and 1938, Sid Luckman blossomed as "The Master of the T-formation" with the National Football League's Chicago Bears. In nine seasons as quarterback of the Bears (1939–47), his "Monsters of the Midway" won four NFL Championships (1940, 1941, 1943, and 1946) and five Western Conference titles. He was named All-Pro five times: 1941–1944 and 1947.

Luckman was the NFL's Most Valuable Player in 1943, the year he threw a single-game record seven touchdowns against the New York Giants. During the Bears' ten-game regular season that year, he threw 28 touchdowns and passed for five more TDs in the Bears' winning NFL Championship game. Luckman's mastery of the then new T-formation system helped "open up" and popularize professional football. In his nine pro seasons, Luckman completed 904 of 1,744 passes, for 14,686 yards (8.42 yards per pass), and 139 touchdowns.

Luckman is a member of the College Football Hall of Fame, and was elected to the Pro Football Hall of Fame in 1965.

Sid Luckman in 1938, his second All-America year at Columbia University.

RON MIX
United States
Born March 10, 1938, in Los Angeles, California

Ron Mix was a ten-time All-League and All-Pro offensive lineman with the American Football League (AFL) San Diego (and Los Angeles) Chargers and Oakland Raiders from 1960 to 1972. A University of Southern California All-America in 1959, he was the first draft choice of both the National Football League Baltimore Colts and the AFL Boston Patriots upon graduation.

The Patriots traded their rights to Mix to the L.A. Chargers in 1960, and one year later the team moved to San Diego, where he played both offensive tackle and offensive guard. He retired in 1970, but returned to play two seasons with the Oakland Raiders. Mix played in a total of seven All-Star games, and when he completed his active career, the Chargers retired his jersey: number 74.

Mix was unanimously named to the All-Time AFL Team by the Pro Football Hall of Fame, who, in 1979, also made Mix the second AFL player and the sixth offensive lineman, all-time, elected to the Pro Football Hall of Fame.

HARRY NEWMAN
United States
Born September 5, 1909, in Detroit, Michigan

The University of Michigan's star triple-threat quarterback, 1930–32, Harry Newman was everybody's All America during his senior year at Ann Arbor. Among his many honors in 1932: the Douglas Fairbanks Trophy as outstanding college player of the season (predecessor of the Heisman Trophy) and the Helms Athletic Foundation "Player of the Year" Award. In his three gridiron seasons at Michigan, the Wolverines won every game, except for two ties and one loss. Of a total of 480 minutes of game time during his undefeated senior year, Newman played 437 minutes. (Players played both offense and defense until the mid-1950s.)

Newman moved to professional football in 1933 with the New York Giants, and was immediately one of the pro game's highest-paid performers, having signed a percentage contract based upon attendance. In his rookie year, he led the Giants to the National Football League championship game against the Chicago Bears. Although the Bears won the contest 23 to 21, Newman tossed two touchdown passes, and at one point completed 13 straight passes. He picked up where he left off the following year, but suffered two broken bones in his back in a mid-season game against the Bears, and his career appeared to be ended. Although the Giants went on to defeat Chicago in the 1934 NFL title game without Newman, the injured quarterback was summoned back from retirement at mid-season 1935, in hopes of reviving the faltering New Yorkers. Newman helped the Giants to the Eastern Conference title that year, but it was to be his final season (only his third) of professional football.

Newman and a Univeristy of Michigan coed celebrate his selection as the nation's number-one All America football star, 1932.

Olympic gold medalist Mitch Gaylord, seen here competing as a member of the UCLA gymnastics team.

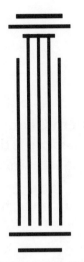 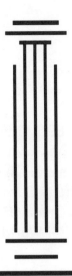

GYMNASTICS

ALFRED FLATOW
Germany
Born 1869 in Berent, Pomerania
Died 1942

Alfred Flatow won four Olympic medals in the first modern Olympiad in Athens, Greece, in 1896—gold medals in Parallel Bars, Team Parallel Bars, and Team Horizontal Bars, and a silver in the Horizontal Bars event.

He is the cousin of Olympian Gustav Felix Flatow. In 1903, Flatow assisted the founding of the Jüdische Turnerschaft, the historic and pioneering Jewish sports organization in Europe. He was prominently active in German gymnastics until being expelled from official competition by the Nazis in 1933.

Flatow is reported to have died in the Theresienstadt concentration camp in 1942. His cousin Gustav Flatow also died in the same camp in 1945.

GUSTAV FELIX FLATOW
United States
Born January 7, 1875, in Berent, Pomerania
Died January 1945

In 1896, Gustav Flatow won two gold medals at the first modern Olympic Games in Athens—in Team Horizontal Bars and Team Parallel Bars. He is the cousin of Olympian Alfred Flatow, who was also a successful medalist at these Athens Games.

Gustav Flatow died in the Theresienstadt concentration camp near the end of World War II.

MITCHELL "MITCH" GAYLORD
United States
Born March 10, 1961, in Los Angeles, California

Gaylord won four medals in the 1984 Los Angeles Olympic Games—a gold in the Team event, a silver in Vaulting, and bronze medals in both Rings and Parallel Bars.

Gaylord saw his first international competition at the 11th Maccabiah Games in 1981, dominating the gymnastics events while winning six gold medals. The only gold medal he did not win was won by his brother, Chuck, who took top honors in the Vault (Mitch won the silver).

MARIA GOROKHOVSKAYA
Soviet Union
Date of birth unknown

Maria Gorokhovskaya was a winner of two gold and five silver medals at the 1952 Olympic Games in Helsinki. With her extraordinary performances, Gorokhovskaya won All-Around and Team gold medals, and silver medals in each of the five other gymnastic events—Vault, Parallel Bars, Balance Beam, Floor Exercise, and Team Hand Apparatus.

Gorokhovskaya emigrated to Israel in early 1990, and it was only then that it became known that she is Jewish.

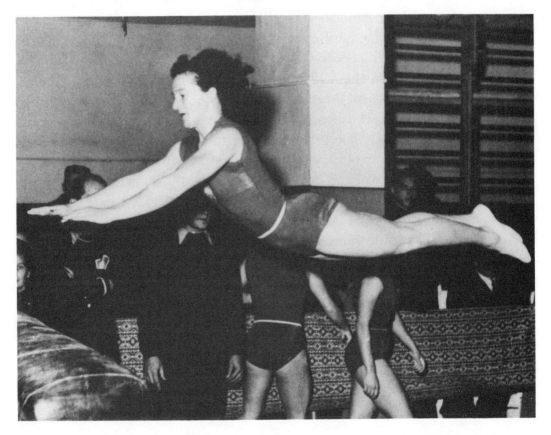

Maria Gorokhovskaya, en route to capturing seven medals at the 1952 Olympic Games.

ABIE GROSSFELD
United States
Born March 1, 1934, in New York City

Abie Grossfeld has represented the United States as a gymnastics competitor or coach in seven Olympic Games, seven World Championships, and five Pan American Games—among numerous other major gymnastics events. He was Head Coach of the United States' Men's Olympic Gymnastics Team in 1972, 1984, and 1988. His 1984 team won the Olympic gold medal. He was also Assistant Coach of U.S. men for the 1964 Olympics and of U.S. women for the 1968 Games. In 1966, 1981, 1983, 1985, and 1987, Grossfeld served as Head Coach of the American Men's World Gymnastics Championships teams. From 1981 to 1988, he was a National Coach of the USA Gymnastics Team. In 1982, he helmed the American World Cup men's team. He head-coached the United States' men's gymnastics teams for two Pan American Games, 1983 and 1987 (in which he won the gold medal), and was Head Coach of the U.S. men competing in the 1986 International Goodwill Games. He also coached U.S. gymnastics for three World Maccabiah Games: 1973, 1977 (men and women), and 1981. His 1981 team won three team gold medals.

As a competitor, Grossfeld competed internationally for the United States for 15 consecutive years, including: the 1956 and 1960 Olympic Games, the World Championships of 1958 and 1962, the Pan American Games of 1955, 1959, and 1963, and the World Maccabiah Games of 1953, 1957, and 1965. Of his 15 Pan Am Games medals, eight were gold—including three Horizontal Bar championships. His Horizontal Bar gold medal record of 1955 stood until 1987—for 32 years! Over his three competitions in the Maccabiah Games, he captured 17 gold medals, including seven in seven events in 1957.

Grossfeld is a 1960 University of Illinois graduate (M.S., 1962). In 1962, he established the first gymnastics program at the United States Coast Guard Academy in New London, Connecticut. Since 1963, he has been a professor of physical education and Head Gymnastics Coach at Southern Connecticut State University. His many honors include: University of Illinois "Athlete of the Year" in 1959; Fédération Internationale de Gymnastique "Master of Sports Award" in 1960; Gymnastics Federation "Coach of the Year" in 1984; the naming of a street in New Haven, Connecticut, ABIE GROSSFELD CIRCLE in 1984; and election to the National Gymnastics Hall of Fame in 1979 for "achievements as a gymnast, coach, and contributor."

Grossfeld on the flying rings.

GEORGE GULACK
United States
Born May 12, 1905, in Riga, Latvia
Date of death unknown

At the 1932 Olympic Games in Los Angeles, George Gulack won a gold medal in Flying Rings. He was the United States Amateur Athletic Union (AAU) Champion in Flying Rings in 1928 and 1935.

Upon completion of his competitive career in 1936, Gulack became a major force on the administrative side of American gymnastics. In 1948, he helped draft a new set of AAU rules designed to conform with international regulations, a major advance in the American national gymnastics program. The same year, he served as manager of the U.S.A. men's and women's Olympic gymnastic teams. A vice-president of the International Gymnastic Federation, Gulack was chairman of both the United States Olympic and National AAU Gymnastic Committees.

AGNES KELETI (Klein)
Hungary
Born June 9, 1921, in Budapest

Agnes Keleti won 11 medals over three Olympiads, including 5 gold medals. At the London Olympic Games in 1948, Keleti won a Team silver medal. In 1952, at Helsinki, she won a gold in the Free-Standing Exercise, a silver in the Combined Team competition, and a bronze each in Hand Apparatus-Team and Uneven Parallel Bars.

At the 1956 Olympic Games in Melbourne, Keleti won gold medals in the Free-Standing Exercise, Balance Beam, Parallel Bars, and Combined Exercise-Team (portable apparatus). She also won silver medals in the Combined Exercise and Combined Exercise-Team.

In 1954, Keleti captured the World Championship in Uneven Bars, and her Hungarian team won the Team Exercises (portable apparatus) World title.

From 1947 to 1956, she won the All-Around Hungarian Championship ten times.

During World War II, Keleti was saved from probable death by Swedish diplomat Raoul Wallenberg. Much of her family, including her father, perished at Auschwitz.

Agnes Keleti is the most successful Jewish female athlete in Olympic history, and ranks as the fourth most successful female Olympian of all-time.

Agnes Keleti performing on the Balance Beam.

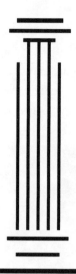

HANDBALL

VICTOR "VIC" HERSHKOWITZ
United States
Born October 5, 1918, in Brooklyn, New York

"As the immortals are recorded in the heroics of Handball, the towering figure of Victor Hershkowitz will stand apart and above all . . ." wrote the United States Handball Association in November 1968.

Beginning in 1942, with the Amateur Athletic Union (AAU) National One-Wall Doubles Championship (with Moe Orenstein), Hershkowitz accumulated 40 national and international titles, including nine straight Three-Wall Singles Championships (1950–58)—a feat no other player has equaled. In 1952, he captured handball's "grandslam": the USHA's Three- and Four-Wall Singles crowns and the AAU One-Wall Singles title.

"The grandslam," comments the *Encyclopedia of Jews in Sports*, "is akin to a baseball pitcher winning 25 games *and* the batting championship during the same year." His Three-Wall Championships from 1950 to 1955 are considered international titles.

In 1954, Vic Hershkowitz was the first handball player to win a career 15th National (U.S.A.) title, and between 1947 and 1967 (except for 1959), he won at least one national championship each year. Jimmy Jacobs (see below), the IJSHOF honoree who shared dominance of the sport with Hershkowitz beginning in 1955, called his senior court star "The Babe Ruth of Handball."

JAMES "JIMMY" JACOBS
United States
Born 1931 in St. Louis, Missouri
Died March 1988

Jimmy Jacobs dominated the sport of four-wall handball from 1955 to 1969, winning every match he played during that 15-year span.

Jacobs won the United States Handball Association Four-Wall Singles and Doubles Championships (with Marty Decatur) six times—the Singles in 1955–1957, 1960, 1964, and 1965. (In 1960 and 1965, he captured both the Singles and Doubles crowns.) He also won the National Three-Wall Championship three times. He did not compete in the National Championships several years, because of either health-injury problems or the lack of meaningful competition. In 1966, *Sports Illustrated* magazine noted that "Jacobs might be the greatest athlete of his time in any sport."

Jimmy Jacobs won every match he played for 15 years. Sports Illustrated wrote that he was possibly "the greatest athlete of his time in any sport."

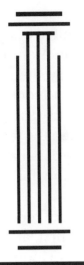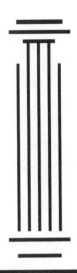

HOCKEY

CECIL "CECE" HART
Canada
Born November 28, 1883, in Bedford Quebec
Died July 1940

A pioneer Canadian sportsman, Cece Hart managed the National Hockey League's Montreal Canadiens to back-to-back Stanley Cup Championships, 1929–30 and 1930–31. He managed the Canadiens for eight full seasons, and in each of those NHL campaigns the Canadiens qualified for the Stanley Cup Playoffs. A direct descendant of Canada's first Jewish settler, Aaron Hart, Cece enjoyed great success from 1900 to 1922, organizing, playing, and managing amateur baseball and hockey teams for the Star Club of Montreal. In 1910, he organized and served as secretary-treasurer of the Montreal City Hockey League, while taking on the responsibilities of secretary-treasurer of the Eastern Canada Amateur Hockey Association.

Shortly before World War I, Hart inaugurated the Art Ross Cup, an international amateur hockey series between Canada and the United States. In 1921, he negotiated a deal for a syndicate to purchase the Montreal Canadiens NHL franchise, and was appointed a club director by the new owners. Three years later, Hart left the Canadiens to manage the new Montreal Maroons NHL franchise, but left after only a few months over a policy dispute. He immediately returned to the Canadiens as a director, but when the team fell to last place, 1925–26 (in a seven-team league), Hart was named manager for the following season. This assignment laid the foundation for the Canadiens NHL dynasty to follow.

In 1926–27, the Hart-led Canadiens catapulted to a second-place regular-season finish, and the following season, 1927–28, they finished first, at one time winning 18 games in a row. The seasons 1929–30 and 1930–31 were to be the big years for Hart and his Canadiens, as they captured back-to-back Stanley Cup championships. His speed and pressure-themed teams were nicknamed the "Flying Frenchmen" and the "Wonder Teams." One season later, however, illness forced Hart to retire from hockey. Coincident to his departure was the decline of the Canadiens' fortunes on ice. When the team dropped to last place during the 1935–36 season, Montreal sportswriters and fans campaigned for Hart's return. Management brought him back for the 1936–37 season, and the Canadiens responded with a first-place regular-season finish. He continued on for another season and a half, until forced out by illness on January 27, 1939.

The National Hockey League's Most Valuable Player of the Year Award, the Hart Trophy, was donated by Hart's father, Dr. David A. Hart, during the 1923–24 season.

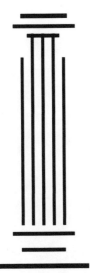

HORSE RACING

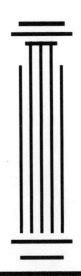

WALTER BLUM
United States
Born 1934 in Brooklyn, New York

Walter Blum won back-to-back American riding championships in 1963 and 1964. In his distinguished 22-year jockey career, Blum rode 4,383 winners. His 1,704 mounts in 1963 were the second highest ever ridden in a single season.

In 1964, Blum was presented the George Woolf Award, an honor given to the jockey whose career has best reflected credit to his profession. In 1974, his 4,000th winning mount made Blum only the sixth United States jockey ever to achieve that level.

Hirsch Jacobs and Walter Blum at Santa Anita in 1964.

HIRSCH JACOBS
United States

Born April 18, 1904, in New York City
Died February 1970

One of horse racing's premier trainers, breeders and owners, Hirsch Jacobs saddled 3,569 winners in his lifetime, more than anyone else in the history of thoroughbred racing.

He was known as the "voodoo veterinarian," having been incredibly successful at turning confirmed losers into winners for nearly 50 years. Unlike other great trainers, Jacobs bred and trained horses he owned, with his career-long partner (since 1931) Isidor "Beebee" Bieber. His finest year was 1936, when he saddled 177 winners.

Some of the horses Jacobs brought into prominence are: Action, Paper Tiger, Hail To Reason, Affectionately, Palestinian, Straight Deal, Regal Gleam and Stymie, a horse he bought for a $1,500 claiming price. Stymie raced 131 times and won $918,485 by the time he retired in 1949—the era's all-time money winner.

Horses Jacobs trained earned more than $12,000,000 in purses. He was the top money-winning trainer in the United States in 1940 and 1960; and he led the United States in total number of yearly winners eleven times, from 1933 to 1944, except in 1940, when he finished second.

Jacobs is a member of the Turf Hall of Fame.

WALTER MILLER
United States

Born 1890 in New York City
Date of death unknown

Walter Miller is recognized as the greatest jockey of the early twentieth century. He rode his first American race in 1904 at the age of 14, and his last in 1909. During a four year period, he had 1,094 winners; and in his career, more than half his mounts finished in the money. In an era when most jockeys seldom went to the post 500 times a year, Miller had 178 winners; out of 888 mounts in 1905; 388 firsts out of 1,384 races in 1906 (and 300 seconds, 199 thirds)—just two years after he learned to ride; 334 wins in 1,194 races in 1907; and 194 winners in 870 mounts in 1908. He won the National Riding Championship in both 1906 and 1907.

Miller enjoyed his greatest success under the James R. Keene Stable colors. He was the first jockey to eclipse 300 winners in one year; and his 388 first-place finishes in 1906 stood alone as the most single-season wins for 44 years. In 1950, Joe Culomex and Willie Shoemaker tied the record, and two years later Shoemaker broke it. It is significant to note that Miller accomplished his extraordinary record in the days of six and seven race cards, and abbreviated racing seasons.

By 1910, Miller had grown too big for American riding, and he opted to race in Europe where he continued to enjoy success. Miller was elected to the Jockey Hall of Fame in 1957.

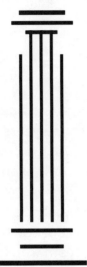

SOCCER

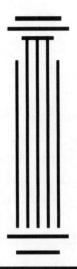

ARTHUR BAAR
Austria
Born 1891
Date of death unknown

Arthur Baar was the leader of the soccer section of the Hakoah of Vienna Sports Club (Austria), and a mentor of the internationally renowned Hakoah-Vienna Soccer Club from 1911 to 1927. He served as Vice-President of Hakoah of Vienna from 1927 to 1938. When Germany annexed Austria in 1938, Baar emigrated to Palestine, where he served as Manager of the Palestine/Israeli National Soccer Team from 1946 to 1954.

BELA GUTTMANN
Hungary
Born 1900 in Budapest
Died August 1981

Bela Guttmann won more honors with world class teams in Europe and South America than any other coach in soccer history. He coached for 30 years in ten different countries, including the national teams of Hungary, Austria, and Portugal. His teams won two European Cups, 10 National Championships, and 7 National Cups.

As a player, 1922–33, he was center-half for the famed Hakoah-Vienna team. He played for them during his entire active career, except for two seasons with an all-Jewish team in New York City. His Hakoah team won the Austrian championship, 1924–26.

HAKOAH-VIENNA CLUB
Austria

Hakoah-Vienna was an all-Jewish soccer club that won Austria's National Championship from 1924 to 1926. This outstanding team attracted Jewish soccer stars from many countries, and gained a worldwide reputation through its many travels. Hakoah-Vienna was the first club to defeat an English team in England, when it decisively romped (5–0) past Great Britain's Westham of London Club in 1923.

Hakoah-Vienna's top players included: Jozsef Eisenhoffer, Sandor Fabian, Richard Fried, Max Gold, Max Grunwald, Jozsef Grunfeld, Bela Guttmann, Alois Hess, Moritz Hausler, "Fuss" Heinrich, Norbert Katz, Alexander Nemes-Neufeld, Egon Pollak, Max Scheuer, Alfred Schoenfeld, Erno Schwarz, Joseph Stross, Jacob Wagner, and Max Wortmann.

Hakoah of Vienna, the parent organization of the famous soccer club, was the largest sporting organization in the world in its time, numbering more than 5,000 members, and offering a wide variety of sports activities.

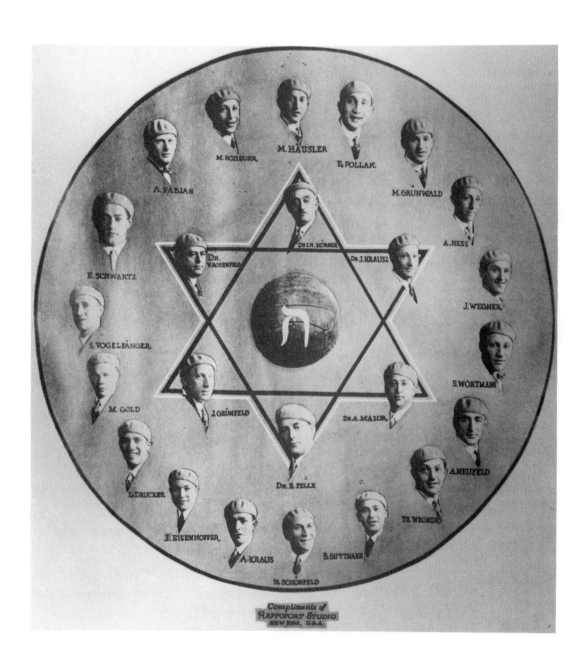

With the rise of Nazism, the Club disbanded in 1938. It reestablished itself after World War II on a modest scale.

GYULA MANDEL
Hungary
Born July 18, 1909, in Budapest
Died November 1969

A member of the Hungarian National Soccer Team for many years, Gyula Mandel became its coach and led the team during its prime years into the 1950s. From 1956 to 1958, Mandel coached the Brazilian National Team; and from 1959 to 1963, he was coach of the Israeli National Team.

HUGO MEISL
Austria
Born 1881 in Czechoslovakia
Died 1937

One of the great soccer authorities in history, Hugo Meisl led the Austrian Soccer Federation as its General Secretary during the 1920s and 1930s. Meisl was Manager and a mentor of the Austrian National "Wunderteam" of the 1930s—the team that set the standard of excellence in world soccer during the era. In 1927, he founded the Mitropa Cup, the first international club competition.

Meisl, a devotee of soccer from early childhood as a player, referee, journalist, and official, has been honored by many European governments, as well as Austria, for his considerable achievements.

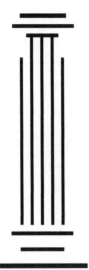

SPEED SKATING

IRVING JAFFEE
United States
Born September 15, 1906, in New York City
Died March 1981

One of America's first great Winter Olympics champions, Irving Jaffee won gold medals in both the 5,000-meter (9:40.8) and 10,000-meter (19:13.6) speed skating events at the 1932 Winter Games in Lake Placid, New York.

Jaffee's unsuccessful quest for an Olympic gold medal in the 10,000-meter event four years earlier had resulted in one of the Winter Games' most lasting controversies. The competition had completed six of eight heats in the 10,000, with Jaffee holding the gold-medal position, having topped Norway's World Champion Bernt Evansen. High temperatures caused the St. Moritz ice to be non-skatable, and in an unprecedented move, the Norwegian referee ruled the competition "no contest." Nonetheless, the International Olympic Committee conferred and overruled the referee, recognizing Jaffee as the event winner. However, soon after, the International Skating Federation overturned the IOC's decision. At the same 1928 Games, Jaffee's fourth-place finish in the 5,000-meter race was the best ever by an American.

Four years later, in 1934, although he had never skated more than 10,000 meters before, Jaffee set the World record in the 25-mile Skating Marathon. He was elected to the United States Skating Hall of Fame in 1940.

Irving Jaffee, America's first Olympic gold-medal speed skater.

SPORTS CONTRIBUTORS

Sir ARTHUR ABRAHAM GOLD
Great Britain
Born January 10, 1917, in London, England

Honorary Secretary of the British Amateur Athletic Board, 1962–77, Arthur Gold served as leader of the British Olympic teams in 1968, 1972, and 1976. In 1976, he was elected Vice-President of the Board and President of the European Track and Field Association. Gold was awarded England's CBE and knighted for his services to athletics.

Sir LUDWIG "POPPA" GUTTMANN
Germany & Great Britain
Born 1899 in Tost, Upper Silesia
Died 1980

Ludwig Guttmann is the father of organized physical activities for the handicapped. He created the Stoke Mandeville Games/Para-Olympics (the Handicapped Olympics).

One of Germany's leading pre-World War II neuro-surgeons, Guttmann fled to England in 1939. In 1944, he was invited by the British government to found and appointed Director of the National Spinal Injuries Center at Stoke Mandeville (near Aylesbury), a position he held until 1966.

The Para-Olympics became international in 1952, and is held every four years, usually following and in the same city as the World Olympic Games. In 1960, Dr. Guttmann founded the British Sports Association of the Disabled. He has received both Great Britain's OBE and CBE, and he has been honored by 18 other nations.

FERENC MEZOE
Hungary
Born March 13, 1885, in Budapest
Died November 1961

Ferenc Mezoe was the first official historian of the Olympic Games. In 1924, he was awarded a gold medal for literature in the Paris Olympic Art Competitions for his book *The Olympic Games in Antiquity*. Mezoe wrote more than 70 works on the Olympics, his first published in 1911. In 1948, he was elected a member of the International Olympic Committee, and served many years as President of the Hungarian Olympic Committee.

ZVI NISHRI (Orloff)
Israel
Born 1878 in Russia
Died July 1973

Zvi Nishri is the father of modern physical education in Palestine/Israel. The Hebrew language owes to Nishri not only its basic terminology of both physical education and sports, but also its first professional publications.

Nishri emigrated to Palestine in 1903, and in 1906, after working as a laborer for several years in Petach Tikvah, became involved in physical education. Two years later, he began teaching, and by 1912 he was training other teachers in physical education. In 1913, Nishri wrote the first of what would be scores of physical education publications—for many years, the only ones authored in Hebrew.

Nishri was also one of the founders of the Maccabi and Scout movements in Palestine. He was professionally active until his death at age 95.

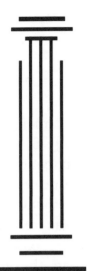 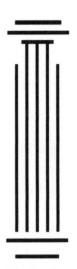

SPORTS MEDIA

MEL ALLEN (Melvin Allen Israel)
United States
Born February 14, 1913, in Birmingham, Alabama

One of the preeminent American sportscasters, Mel Allen is most famous as the radio and television "Voice of the New York Yankees" baseball team from 1939 to 1964. He also broadcast New York Giant baseball games from 1939 to 1943, 20 World Series, 14 Rose Bowl games, two Orange Bowls, two Sugar Bowls, and 24 All-Star baseball games.

Allen came out of retirement in 1981, and continues as the cable TV "Voice of the Yankees" and host of the long-running series *This Week in Baseball*.

A recipient of numerous industry, listener, and viewer awards, Allen was one of the first elected to the National (USA) Sportswriters and Broadcasters Hall of Fame in March 1972, and was presented with the Ford Frick Award in 1978 on his election to Baseball's Hall of Fame.

Mel Allen, the "Voice of the New York Yankees."

Mark Spitz, the greatest competitive swimmer in history.

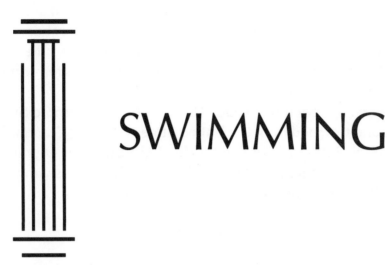
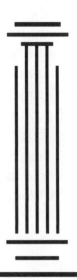

SWIMMING

CHARLOTTE "EPPIE" EPSTEIN
United States
Born 1885 in New York City
Died August 1938

The "mother" of American women's swimming, Charlotte Epstein established it as a recognized sport in the United States, and was responsible for its inclusion on the 1920 Antwerp Olympic Games program.

In October 1914, Epstein founded the National Women's Life Saving League (later changed to the New York Women's Swimming Association, or WSA). Within months, she persuaded the U.S. Amateur Athletic Union to permit women swimmers, for the first time, to register as athletes with the AAU.

A court stenographer by trade, Epstein headed the United States lady swimmers at the 1920, 1924, and 1932 Olympiads. During this time, American female swimmers dominated the Games. Among the swimmers considered her protégés were Gertrude Ederle, Aleen Riggin, and Eleanor Holm.

The success of the American female swim team at the Antwerp Olympics led to the establishment of other events for female athletes—in track and field and other sports—at future Olympic Games. (*Note:* Women's archery and golf, which had appeared in 1900 and 1904, had previously been the only events available to female athletes. In 1928, track and field events for women were introduced for the first time.)

Epstein was invited to coach the 1936 U.S.A. Women's Olympic Swim Team, but declined and resigned from the United States Olympic Committee in protest against Nazi Germany's policies. (The 1936 Summer Olympics were held in Berlin.) During her 22 years with the WSA, Epstein's swimmers set 51 World records and registered 31 national championships.

ALFRED HAJOS-GUTTMANN
Hungary
Born February 1, 1878, in Budapest
Died November 1955

Competing in Athens at the first modern Olympic Games in 1896, Alfred Hajos-Guttmann was the first-ever Olympic swimming champion, and the first Hungarian Olympic gold medalist. He won two swimming gold medals in Athens, in the 100-Meter Freestyle (1:22.2) and 1,200-Meter Freestyle (18:22.2). Hajos-Guttmann was 100-Meter European Swimming Champion in 1895 and 1896.

In later years, Hajos-Guttmann became a world renowned architect specializing in sport facilities. In a special arts competition at the 1924 Paris Olympic Games, he was awarded an Olympic silver medal for architecture — the highest honor given in that competition. He is also a recipient of the Olympic Diploma of Merit.

A versatile athlete, Hajos-Guttmann was Hungary's National 100-Meter Sprint (track) Champion in 1898, as well as 400-Meter Hurdles and Discus Champion. He also played forward on Hungary's national soccer championship teams of 1901, 1902, and 1903.

OTTO HERSCHMANN
Austria
Born January 4, 1877, in Vienna
Date of death unknown

Dr. Otto Herschmann is one of only three athletes to have gained Olympic medals in two different Olympic sports. He won a bronze medal swimming the 100-meter Freestyle at the first modern Olympic Games (Athens) in 1896, and a silver medal for fencing in Team Sabre at the 1912 Olympics in Stockholm.

Coincidentally, Herschmann also served as President of the Austrian Olympic Committee during the 1912 Games, thus becoming the only president of a National Olympic Committee to win an Olympic medal while in office.

Dr. Herschmann perished in the concentration camp of Izbica, Yugoslavia, during World War II.

PAUL NEUMANN
Austria & United States
Born June 13, 1875, in Vienna
Date of death unknown

Paul Neumann won a gold medal in the 500-Meter Freestyle (8:12.6) in 1896, at the first modern Olympic Games in Athens, Greece. Neumann first gained swimming notoriety in 1892, when he won Austria's National River Swimming Championship.

Following the Athens Olympiad, Neumann emigrated to the United States as a University of Chicago medical student. Competing for the Chicago Athletic Association in 1897, he set World Records in the Two-, Three-, Four-, and Five-Mile Swimming events. The same year, he also won the American and Canadian National Freestyle Championships.

MARILYN RAMENOFSKY
United States
Born August 20, 1946, in Phoenix, Arizona

Marilyn Ramenofsky set the World Record for the 400-Meter Freestyle three times in 1964, lowering the mark to 4:39.5. She captured a silver medal in the 400 at the Tokyo Olympics that same year. She also set the American Record in the 220-Meter Freestyle in 1964: 2:17.3.

The 1961 Maccabiah Games were her introduction to international competition, and she won a gold medal in the 400-Meter Freestyle Relay, as well as a bronze in the 400-Meter Freestyle. Ramenofsky returned to Israel for the 1965 Maccabiah to win gold medals in both the 220- and 400-Meter Freestyles.

She was named to the 1962, 1963, and 1964 All-American Women's Amateur Athletic Union (AAU) Swimming Teams.

MARK SPITZ
United States
Born February 10, 1950, in Modesto, California

Mark Spitz is the greatest competitive swimmer in history, and holder of the most extraordinary achievement in Olympic Games history: the winning of seven gold medals in one Olympiad. Spitz won 11 medals over two Olympic Games, but will always be remembered best for his remarkable seven-gold feat at the 1972 Games in Munich. That summer in Munich, Spitz set four individual World Records—100-Meter (51.22) and 200-Meter Freestyle (1:52.78), 100-Meter (54.27), and 200-Meter Butterfly (2:00.70)—and participated in three World relay records.

His final victory came only hours before Palestinian terrorists took hostage and eventually murdered 11 Israeli athletes in the Munich Olympic Village. Spitz was unceremoniously whisked out of the country under heavy security guard.

Four years earlier, Spitz won "only" four Olympic medals at the Mexico Games: golds in two relay events, a silver in the 100-Meter Relay, and a bronze in the 100-Meter Freestyle. Between 1965 and 1972, he won nine Olympic gold medals, one silver and one bronze...five Pan-American Games golds...31 National (U.S.A.) Amateur Athletic Union (AAU) titles ...and eight National Collegiate Athletic Association (NCAA) championships. During those years, he set 33 World Records.

He was "World Swimmer of the Year" in 1967, 1971, and 1972. In 1971, Spitz became the first Jewish recipient of the James E. Sullivan Award, given annually to the Amateur Athlete of the Year.

His first international competition came at the 1965 Maccabiah Games. Spitz returned to Israel in 1969, following the Mexico Olympiad, to again compete in the Maccabiah. In all, he won 10 Maccabiah gold medals.

EVA SZEKELY
Hungary
Born April 3, 1927, in Budapest

Eva Szekely set ten World and five Olympic swimming records. She set an Olympic record in the 200-Meter Breastroke (2:51.7) en route to a gold medal at the 1952 Helsinki Games, and captured a silver medal in the same event at the Melbourne Olympics in 1956. Szekely was fourth in the 200-Meter Breaststroke at the 1948 London Games.

Among her World Records: 100-meter Breaststroke (1:16.9), set May 1951 . . . 400-Meter Freestyle Relay Team (4:27.2), set in May 1952 . . . 400-Meter Individual Medley (5:50.4), set in April 1953. She also earned ten World University Championships and 68 Hungarian national titles.

Szekely became victim of the sweeping anti-Jewish sentiment of the early 1940s when she was expelled from her local team as a "religious undesirable." During 1944–45, she lived with her family in a Swiss-run "safe house" in Budapest.

Szekely turned to a successful career in coaching following her competitive days. One of her most successful young swimmers was her daughter Andrea, who won a silver medal at the 1972 Munich Olympics in the 100-Meter Back-stroke, and a bronze in the 100-Meter Butterfly—establishing a World record while taking first place in her semi-final heat.

Eva Szekely, Hungary's great swimming champion of the 1950s.

TABLE TENNIS

ANGELICA ADELSTEIN-ROZEANU
Romania
Born October 15, 1921, in Bucharest

Angelica Adelstein-Rozeanu is considered the greatest female table tennis player in history. She won 17 World titles, including six Straight Singles Championships, 1950–55. She also won the World women's doubles title twice, the World mixed doubles crown three times, and led the Romanian National Team to five Corbillon Cup victories. (The Corbillon Cup is presented to the world's best women's table tennis team.) Rozeanu was the first Romanian woman to win a World title in any sport.

She first won the Romanian National Women's Championship in 1936, and captured it every year until 1957 (excluding the war years, 1940–45, when she did not compete). From 1950 to 1960, Adelstein-Rozeanu served as President of the Romanian Table Tennis Commission, and in 1954 was presented the highest sports distinction in Romania: the title of Merited

Master of Sport. She also received four Order of Work honors from her government. Rozeanu moved to Israel in 1960, and in 1961 won the Maccabiah Games table tennis championship.

VIKTOR BARNA (Braun)
Hungary
Born August 24, 1911, in Budapest
Died February 1972

Viktor Barna won 23 World Championship titles, including five Singles, eight Doubles, three Mixed-Doubles, and seven Team titles. He has been described by Sir Ivor Montagu, President of the International Table Tennis Association, as "the greatest table tennis player who ever lived."

In 1929, Barna was a member of the Hungarian National Team that won the Swaythling Cup, symbolic of the Men's World Team Championship. One year later, he won the first of his five World Singles Championships. Barna's greatest performance came in February 1935, at the World Championships in Wembley, England, when he captured the World Singles, Doubles, and Mixed-Doubles crowns. Later that year, his Hungarian National Team was again awarded the Swaythling Cup.

In May 1935, Barna's championship career was effectively ended when his right (playing) arm was severely injured in an auto accident.

Viktor Barna, holder of 23 World Championship table tennis titles.

RICHARD BERGMANN
Austria & Great Britain
Born 1920 in Vienna
Died 1970

A winner of seven World Championships, including four Singles crowns, Richard Bergmann was regarded as the greatest defensive player in table tennis history.

In 1936, he won his first World title as a member of the Hungarian Swaythling Cup (World Championship) Team. He won his first World Singles Championship in 1937, and in doing so became the youngest player ever to win the title.

One year later, when the Nazis invaded Austria, Bergmann fled to England. In 1939, he won his second World Singles Championship, as well as the World Doubles title (pairing with Viktor Barna). He reclaimed his title as World Singles Champion in 1948, and won it again in 1950. His last World crown came as a member of the 1953 British Swaythling Cup Team.

In the mid-1950s, Bergmann became the world's first professional table tennis player, and toured extensively with the Harlem Globetrotters basketball team.

IVOR GOLDSMID MONTAGU
Great Britain
Born April 23, 1904, in London, England

As a result of his efforts, table tennis became an international sport. In 1926, Ivor Montagu initiated the creation of the International Table Tennis Association, and served as its first president for 36 years, until 1962. At age 18, he was a founder of the English Table Tennis Association, and served as its president from 1922 to 1931, and from 1958 to 1965.

Since 1926, the trophy presented annually to the men's World Champion table tennis team bears the name The Swaythling Cup—named for Montagu's mother, Lady Gladys Goldsmid Montagu Swaythling.

MIKLOS SZABADOS
Hungary
Dates of birth and death unknown

Miklos Szabados was the winner of 15 World Championship titles, including the World Singles crown in 1931. From 1928 to 1935, Szabados captured six World titles in doubles (with Viktor Barna), and five times (1929, 1930, 1931, 1934, and 1935) was a member of the Hungarian World Championship (Swaythling Cup) Team. In 1930, 1931, and 1934, Szabados won World titles in mixed doubles.

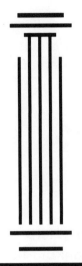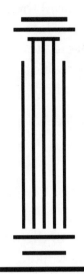

TENNIS

ANGELA BUXTON
Great Britain
Born August 16, 1934, in Liverpool, England

The first British woman to reach a Wimbledon final in 17 years, Angela Buxton captured the Wimbledon Doubles Championship (with Althea Gibson) in 1956.

October 1953 marked a turning point in Buxton's then modest playing career when she won the Maccabiah Games Singles title, easily defeating number 8 World seed Anita Kanter (U.S.A.), who had recently beaten number 1 World seed Doris Hart.

Inspired by her success in Israel, Buxton was able to achieve a number 4 English ranking in 1954, and in 1955 reached the Wimbledon Singles quarterfinals and a number 9 World ranking. 1956 was her best year, winning the Wimbledon Doubles, reaching the Wimbledon Singles finals, taking the English Indoor and Grass Court Singles Championships, the English

Hardcourt and Doubles crown (with Darlene Hard), and winning (with Althea Gibson) the French Open Doubles title.

In late 1956, the year of her Wimbledon victory, Buxton suffered a severe wrist injury. Although she still managed to win the French and Maccabiah Singles titles a year later, her playing career was prematurely curtailed.

HERB FLAM
United States
Born November 7, 1928, in New York City
Date of death unknown

One of the world's outstanding tennis players from 1951 to 1957, Herb Flam was ranked in the World's Top Ten four times, his highest ranking being number 5 (World Tennis) in 1957. He ranked in the U.S. Top Ten, 1948–58 (except during Navy service, 1953–54), earning the number 2 spot in 1950, 1956, and 1958.

Flam first gained attention in 1943, when he won the United States Lawn Tennis Association 15-year-old Boys Championship Singles. As a Beverly Hills High School Junior in 1945, he captured the USLTA Interscholastic Singles and Doubles (with Hugh Stewart) titles. The pair won the Doubles crown again in 1946. Flam earned national prominence in 1948, when he entered the USLTA Singles Championships unseeded and reached the tournament semi-finals, en route defeating third and sixth seeds Gardner Mulloy and Harry Likas. The achievement earned the 20-year-old UCLA undergrad a number 9 USA ranking. In 1950, the year he won the USLTA Intercollegiate Singles and Doubles (with Gene Garrett) titles, Flam reached the finals of the USLTA National Singles, becoming the first Jewish tennis player ever to advance to the championship round. (He lost to Art Larsen in five sets.) Nonetheless, he won the United States National Clay Court Singles in 1950, and teamed with Larsen to win the Clay Court Doubles crown as well. (Flam took the Clay Court Singles Championship again in 1956.) On his return from U.S. Navy service in 1955, he won the U.S. National Hardcourt Championship.

Flam reached the Wimbledon Singles semi-finals in 1952, the final eight at Wimbledon three times, and six times reached the quarter-finals of the National Singles. Competing in his first Davis Cup matches for the United States in 1951, and last in 1957, Flam won 12 of 14 contests.

DICK SAVITT
United States
Born March 4, 1927, in Bayonne, New Jersey

In 1951, Dick Savitt won the Wimbledon Singles Championship, the Australian Singles crown, and was named to the United States Davis Cup Team. In his prime, he was considered the greatest backcourt player in the game, and held the number 3 ranking worldwide in 1951 *(World Tennis* magazine).

But Savitt abruptly retired from competitive tennis just one year later, after winning the U.S. National Indoor Singles Championship. Although he has never publicly discussed his retirement, it was considered most likely the result of a never explained snub by the U.S. Davis Cup coaching staff.

Savitt had played and won his early 1951 Cup matches en route to helping position the American team into the Championship Round against Australia. His coaches, however, did not permit Savitt to compete against the Aussies, who, only months earlier, he had dominated both at Wimbledon and in Australia. He had trounced the number 1 Australian (Ken McGregor) at Wimbledon in three straight sets, and in Australia Savitt was the first non-Aussie to win that title in 13 years. Without Savitt's participation, the United States lost the 1951 Davis Cup to the Australians.

Savitt returned to the competitive tennis scene part-time in 1956, and even though his limited tournament competition prevented him from receiving an official ranking, he was nonetheless considered the number 1 player in the United States.

Among the titles captured by Savitt were the 1958 and 1961 U.S. National Indoor Championships—making him the first to win that crown three times.

In 1961, Savitt won both the Singles and Doubles (with Mike Franks) Championships at the World Maccabiah Games in Israel.

Harold Abrahams, whose Olympic and personal deeds were captured in the Oscar-winning film Chariots of Fire.

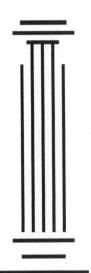
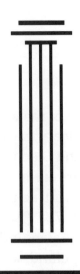

TRACK
AND FIELD

HAROLD MAURICE ABRAHAMS
Great Britain
Born December 15, 1899, in Bedford, England
Died January 1978

Abrahams won a gold medal in the 100-Meter Dash at the Paris Olympic Games of 1924, equaling the Olympic record of 10.6. He was the first non-American to capture the event. At the same Paris Games, he also won a silver medal, leading off the 4x100-Meter Relay for Great Britain, and finished sixth in the 200-meter event. Both his Olympic and personal stories are chronicled in the Academy Award-winning motion picture *Chariots of Fire*.

One year after the 1924 Olympiad, a serious leg injury cut short his competitive career. Nonetheless, he further distinguished himself as a sports journalist, broadcaster, and leader of Great Britain's amateur sports establishment.

LILLIAN COPELAND
United States
Born November 25, 1905, in New York City
Died July 1964

One of the world's great female athletes, Lillian Copeland capped her extraordinary track and field career in 1932, when she won an Olympic gold medal in the Discus Throw, setting a World record of 133′2″ (40.58 meters). Four years earlier, at the Olympic Games in Amsterdam—the first to include women's track and field—Copeland had won a silver medal in the Discus: 121′7⅞″ (37.08 meters).

As an undergraduate student at the University of Southern California, Copeland, who excelled at tennis and basketball, won every women's track and field event she entered. She captured the first of her nine United States National Championships in 1925 with a victory in the 8-Pound Shotput. A year later, Copeland established herself as one of the world's premier women athletes when she won a trio of National titles in the shotput, discus, and javelin. Her victories in the Javelin, 112′5½″ (34.28 meters), and Discus, 101′1″ (30.81 meters), set new World Records. In 1927, she raised her World Javelin mark to 125′8½″ (38.32 meters). In 1928, she upped the World Shotput record to 40′4¼″ (12.30 meters).

Disappointed that her best event, the 8-Pound Shotput, was not included on the 1928 Olympic program, Copeland instead entered the discus event. Nevertheless, at the U.S. Olympic trials, Copeland set a World Discus record of 115′8½″ (35.27 meters), and ran the lead-off leg on the World Record-setting United States 440-Yard Relay Team (50.0). Between 1925 and 1932, Copeland set six World Records, *each,* in the shotput, javelin, and discus throw.

In 1935, she was a member of the second-ever United States Maccabiah Games Team, and won gold medals in each of her specialty events. In the heat of an international controversy concerning a boycott of the 1936 Olympic Games in Berlin, Copeland was one of many Olympic stars who opted not to compete in Nazi Germany.

American track and field champion Lillian Copeland, who won a silver medal for discus throwing at the Amsterdam Olympic Games in 1928—the first Games to include women's athletics—and won a gold in Los Angeles in 1932.

LILLI HENOCH
Germany
Born October 26, 1899, in Königsberg, East Prussia
Date of death unknown

Lilli Henoch set the World Discus record on October 1, 1922, in Berlin, with a throw of 24.90 meters, and bettered that mark on July 8, 1923 (also in Berlin), with a distance of 26.62 meters. On August 16, 1925, in Leipzig, she set the World Shotput record with a toss of 11.57 meters. A year later, Henoch ran the first leg of the foursome (Henoch-Poting-Voss-Kohler) that set a new World Record for the 4x100-Meter Relay—50.4 seconds—at the German tournaments in Cologne. Between 1922 and 1926, she won 10 German National Championships: Shotput (1922–25), Discus (1923 and 1924), Long Jump (1924), and 4x100- Meter Relay (1924–26).

Henoch died in a Nazi concentration camp during World War II.

MARIA ITKINA
Soviet Union
Born in May 3, 1932, Smolensk, Russia

Maria Itkina was among the world's leading sprinters in 100- to 400-Meter events during the 1950s and 1960s.

Itkina established a 400-Meter World Record of 53.9 seconds in 1955, and subsequently tied or broke that mark six times, eventually lowering the record to 53.0 on August 29, 1964. In July 1956, she clocked a World Record 23.6 in the 220-Yard event; and, in September 1959, set the World 440-Yard record at 53.7.

In 1963, Itkina ran the third leg of the Soviet women's 800-Meter relay team that established a World record of 1:34.7. Itkina's mark of 11.4 in the 100-Meters ranks her among the best-ever at the distance. She has also set multiple European sprint records and holds 17 Russian track and field titles.

Itkina is a Merited Master of Sports in the Soviet Union, the highest national honor bestowed on Soviet athletes.

ELIAS KATZ
Finland
Born 1901 in Åbo (Turku)
Died December 1947

Elias Katz won a gold medal at the 1924 Paris Olympic Games as a member of Finland's 3,000-Meter Cross-Country Team. Their championship time was 8:32.0. (His teammates included the legendary Paavo Nurmi and Willie Ritola.) He also won a silver medal in the 3,000-Meter Steeplechase at the Paris Games, clocking 9:44.0. Earlier, Katz had established an Olympic record, 9:43.8, in his first heat in the event. His best time in the 3,000-Meter Steeplechase was 9:40.9, in 1923.

Katz ran the second leg on his Finnish club's 4x1,500 Relay Team that set two World Records—the first, 16:26.2 in July 1926; and the second later that same year, lowering the mark to 16:11.4. In 1925, Bar Kochba of Berlin, the first Jewish national sports club in Central Europe (founded in 1898), invited Katz to represent the club. He did, but returned to his native Finland two years later to prepare for the 1928 Olympic Games.

When a severe foot injury ended his chances to compete in the Amsterdam Olympiad, Katz returned to Germany and Bar Kochba. His presence encouraged many outstanding German Jewish athletes to join the Club, which flourished until forced to disband by the Nazis in the early 1930s.

Katz emigrated to Palestine in 1933, and was selected to coach the first Israeli Olympic track team for the 1948 Games in London. Neither he nor the Israeli team, however, ever got to England. Israel was not admitted into the Olympic family until the 1952 Olympic Games, and Katz was murdered by Arab terrorists in December 1947, while working as a film projectionist at a British army camp near Gaza.

Elias Katz runs for Bar Kochba

IRENA KIRSZENSTEIN-SZEWINSKA
Poland
Born May 24, 1946, in Leningrad, Soviet Union

One of the greatest women track and field athletes of all time, Irena Kirszenstein-Szewinska won medals in four consecutive Olympic Games, a feat never accomplished before by any runner, male or female.

Eighteen years old at the 1964 Tokyo Olympics, Kirszenstein won a gold medal as a member of Poland's World Record-setting 400-Meter Relay Team (43.6), a silver medal in the 200-Meter Dash (her mark of 23.1 set the European record in the event), and a silver medal in the Long Jump.

In Mexico City in 1968, now Kirszenstein-Szewinska, Irena won a gold medal in the 200-Meter event, setting a new World record of 22.5, while breaking her own World Record set three years earlier. She also took a bronze medal in the 100-meter event. After giving birth to a son in 1970, Kirszenstein-Szewinska won bronze medals in the 200-Meter Sprint at the 1971 European Championships and the 1972 Olympics in Munich.

In 1974, she changed to the 400-meter event, and was the first woman to break 50 seconds at that distance. Two years later, at the 1976 Montreal Olympics, Kirszenstein-Szewinska set the World Record at 49.29, as she captured the gold medal in the 400-Meter Sprint.

In all, Kirszenstein-Szewinska won seven Olympic medals (three gold) and ten European medals (five gold), a record unequalled in the history of women's track and field. Other highlights of her extraordinary career include: Tying the 100-Meter World Record in 1965 at 11.1; in 1974, lowering her own World Record in the 200-meter event to 22.0; in 1977, lowering her 400-Meter World Record to 49.0 at the World Championships in Düsseldorf.

Irena Kirszenstein-Szewinska was Poland's Athlete of the Year in 1965. That same year, *Tass*, the official Soviet press agency, named her Outstanding Woman Athlete in the World. In addition, she was *World Sport* magazine's Sportswoman of the Year in 1966, the United Press International (UPI) Sportswoman of 1974, and 1974 *Track and Field News* Woman Athlete of the Year.

Irena Kirszenstein-Szewinska sets a World record in 1968 as she sprints to an Olympic gold medal in the 200-Meter in Mexico City.

ABEL KIVIAT
United States
Born June 23, 1892, in New York City

Abel Kiviat won a silver medal at the 1912 Stockholm Olympic Games in the 1,500-Meter Run (3:59.9). Three years earlier, at the age of 17, he established his first World Record, 2:47.2, in the Two-thirds-Mile Run. The previous mark had stood for 21 years. On June 2, 1912, Kiviat broke the World record in the 1,500 meter, clocking 3:56.8; and six days later lowered that record to 3:55.8 at the United States Olympic trials. That mark stood as a World record for five years, and as a U.S. record until 1928.

Kiviat established himself as one of the great indoor distance runners of all-time in 1911, when the 5'5"/110-pound trackster won both the United States Amateur Athletic Union 600-Yard and 1,000-Yard Indoor Championships. It was the first time the two events had ever been won by the same person. In 1913, he repeated his AAU "double"—this time capturing both victories on the same night! That same year, he demonstrated his versatility by winning the American Six-Mile Cross-Country title and establishing the United States Indoor One-Mile record of 4:18.2.

FANIA MELNIK
Soviet Union
Born June 9, 1945, in Bakota, Ukraine

Fania Melnik set 11 World Discus records during her career. One of the world's greatest female discus throwers, Melnik set her first World mark with a throw of 64.22 meters in her international debut at the 1971 European Championships. A year later, at the Munich Olympic Games, she captured the gold medal as she bettered her World Discus record and re-set the Olympic record three times, with a final mark of 66.62 meters.

During the next four years, Melnik bettered her World record several more times. Although she managed only a fourth place finish at the 1976 Olympics in Montreal, she had her best career throw that year, a toss of 70.50 meters—a record-breaking throw that made her the first woman to exceed the 70-meter mark. In 1977, she won the first World Cup Discus competition in Düsseldorf, Germany.

LAURENCE E. "LON" MYERS
United States
Born February 16, 1858, in Richmond, Virginia
Died February 1899

The greatest short-distance runner of the 19th century, Lon Myers was the first to run the quarter-mile in less than 50 seconds (49.2). From 1880 to 1888,

Myers held the World record for the 100-Yard, 440-Yard, and the 880-Yard events. His best event was the Quarter-Mile (the 440), which he lowered from 50.4 to 48.8. At one time or another over a 21-year period, Myers held all American records for races 50 yards to one mile! He also held ten Canadian and three British national championships.

Myers ran more 880s under two minutes and more 440s under 50 seconds than the total run by all amateur and professional athletes of his era. In the 1879 National (United States) Amateur Athletic Union Championships, he won a triple victory (220, 440, 880), setting records in each event. In 1880, he won four titles in the AAUs: the 220, 440, and 880 events and the 100-Yard Dash—a feat he repeated just one week later at the Canadian Nationals. Myers was the first and probably the only track and field athlete ever to capture eight National titles in one week.

MYER PRINSTEIN
United States
Born 1880 in Russia
Died March 1928

A five-time Olympic medalist (four golds), Myer Prinstein won his first gold medal in the 1900 Triple Jump with a leap of 47' 5¾" (14.47 meters). He also took a silver medal in the Long Jump at the 1900 Paris Olympics, with a mark of 23' 6½" (7.175 meters). In 1904, at the St. Louis Olympiad, Prinstein captured gold medals in both the Long Jump, setting an Olympic record with 24' 1" (7.34 meters), and the Triple Jump, with a mark of 47' 1" (14.35 meters). At the Athens Olympics of 1906, Prinstein again took gold-medal honors in the Long Jump, with a leap of 23' 7½" (7.20 meters).

In addition to his Olympic honors, Prinstein also won many United States track titles, his first in 1898. In 1900, he set the World Long Jump record of 24' 7¼" (7.50 meters), nearly three inches beyond the previous mark.

Prinstein's lone non-gold Olympic medal (a silver) was the subject of controversy at the 1900 Games. At the completion of the Long Jump trials, on Saturday, he was leading the competition. The finals were to be held on

Sunday. As a Syracuse University student, Prinstein was obliged, along with many other American student athletes, not to compete on Sunday, the Christian sabbath (Syracuse is a Methodist school). While he did as instructed, a few American athletes did compete on that Sunday, including his Long Jump arch-rival, the University of Pennsylvania's Alvin Kraenzlein. In Prinstein's absence, with six unchallenged leaps, Kraenzlein managed to top Prinstein's previous-day heading mark to win the gold medal.

The Philadelphia Relay Team of 1901. Left to right: Harry L. Gardner, Foster S. Post, Justus M. Scrafford, and Myer Prinstein (Captain).

FANNY "BOBBIE" ROSENFELD
Canada
Born December 28, 1903, in Katrinaslov, Russia
Died December 1969

In 1950, Bobbie Rosenfeld was selected as Canada's Female Athlete of the Half-Century by the sportswriters of Canada. At the 1928 Olympic Games in Amsterdam—the first in which women athletes participated—Rosenfeld won a gold medal as lead-off leg of the Canadian World record-setting 400-Meter Relay Team (48.4). She also won a silver medal in the 100-Meter Sprint.

In 1922, while excelling in basketball, softball, tennis, and ice hockey, Rosenfeld decided to devote herself primarily to track and field. Three years later, she equaled the World Record of 11.0 in the 100-Yard Dash. During her career, she held a variety of Canadian records in the standing long jump, the running long jump, the 8-pound shotput, the discus, and the javelin. And, in 1924, she won the Toronto Ladies Grass Court Tennis Championship.

Rosenfeld is a member of the Canadian AAU Hall of Fame.

WATER POLO

GYÖRGY BRODY
Hungary
Born July 2, 1908
Died August 1967

György Brody is considered one of the greatest water polo goalies of all time. His Hungarian teams won gold medals at the 1932 Los Angeles and 1936 Berlin Olympic Games. A member of the 1928 Hungarian National Championship Team, Brody played with the team 74 times during his career. His 1934 National team won the European Championship.

BELA KOMJADI
Hungary
Born 1892 in Budapest
Died in 1933

The most innovative water polo coach of his time, Béla Komjadi is credited with the development of Hungary as a World water polo power. He coached his Hungarian National Team to an Olympic silver medal in 1928, and they returned to win the gold medal four years later, at the 1932 Los Angeles Olympic Games. "Uncle Komi" died in 1933, at the age of only 41. At the highly charged Berlin Olympics in 1936, four of the six starters and several reserves from the 1932 championship team led Hungary to a repeat gold-medal victory. Returning home from Germany, the Olympic water polo team held a memorial salute to their coach at his graveside.

(There appear to be no extant photographs or other likenesses of Komjadi.)

MIKLOS SARKANY
Hungary
Born in Budapest
Dates of birth and death unknown

Sarkany won gold medals at both the 1932 and 1936 Olympic Games as a member of the Hungarian Championship Water Polo Teams.

WEIGHTLIFTING

ISAAC "IKE" BERGER
United States
Born November 16, 1936, in Jerusalem, Palestine

Ike Berger is three-time World Featherweight Weightlifting Champion, winner of three Olympic medals, holder of 23 World Weightlifting records, and 12-time United States National titleholder.

The son of a rabbi and himself an ordained cantor, Berger was the first featherweight in history to lift more than 800 pounds, and the first to press double his body weight. In the featherweight class, he won a gold medal at the 1956 Olympic Games in Melbourne (776½ lbs./352.5 kgs.), a silver in 1960 at the Rome Olympiad (798¾ lbs./362.6 kgs.), and a silver at the Tokyo Games in 1964 (841½ lbs./382.5 kgs.). His 1964 Olympic record of 336 pounds in the jerk, at a body-weight of 130 pounds, made him pound-for-pound the strongest man in the world—a record that stood for nine years. He was undefeated in six competitions against the Soviet Union.

Competing in the Fifth Maccabiah Games in 1957, the year after winning his Olympic gold medal, Berger became the first athlete to establish a World Record in the State of Israel, pressing 258 pounds (117.1 kgs.) in Featherweight competition.

In 1965, he was elected to the United States Weightlifters Hall of Fame.

Ike Berger

EDWARD LAWRENCE LEVY
Great Britain
Born December 21, 1851, in London, England
Died May 1932

In March 1891, in open competition against champions from Germany, Belgium, Austria, and Italy, Edward Levy won the first World Weightlifting Competition. The three-day event consisted primarily of repetition and alternate pressing with 56 or 84 pounds in each hand. Just two months earlier, at the age of 40, he won the first British Amateur Weightlifting Championship.

Between 1891 and 1894, Levy set 14 World records. In 1896, at the first modern Olympics in Athens, he served as a member of the International Weightlifting Jury. He is founder of the Amateur Gymnastics Federation of Great Britain and Ireland.

GRIGORI NOVAK
Soviet Union
Born March 5, 1919, in Chernobyl, Ukraine
Died in 1980

Grigori Novak is the holder of 55 World Weightlifting records. He won the World Light-Heavyweight Championship in 1946 (936½ lbs.), and captured a silver medal at the 1952 Helsinki Olympic Games in the Middle-Heavyweight division (903¾ lbs./410 kgs.).

FRANK SPELLMAN
United States
Born September 17, 1922, in Paoli, Pennsylvania

Frank Spellman won a gold medal at the 1948 Olympic Games in London, establishing an Olympic record—860 lbs./390 kgs.—in the Middleweight Division. He enjoyed a long and successful career as a weightlifter, winning many United States National titles, his last in 1971, at the age of 49.

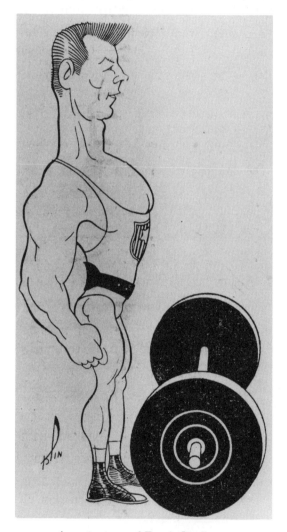

A caricature of Frank Spellman.

WRESTLING

BORIS MENDELOVITCH GUREVICH
Soviet Union
Born March 23, 1931

Boris Mendelovitch Gurevich was the winner of a gold medal in the Flyweight Division of Greco-Roman Wrestling at the 1952 Olympics in Helsinki. He went on to capture World Championship titles in the same event in 1953 and 1955.

BORIS MICHAIL GUREVITCH
Soviet Union
Born February 2, 1937, in Kiev, Ukraine

Boris Michail Gurevitch was the Olympic Freestyle Middleweight (82 kgs.) gold medalist at the 1968 Mexico Games.

RICHARD WEISZ
Hungary
Born 1879 in Budapest
Died in 1945

At the 1908 Olympics in London, Richard Weisz won a gold medal in the Greco-Roman Heavyweight class. The possessor of a 20-inch neck and a 50-inch chest, Weisz was Hungarian National Heavyweight Champion from 1903 to 1909. He was also an outstanding weightlifter.

HENRY WITTENBERG
United States
Born September 18, 1918, in Jersey City, New Jersey

One of the World's all-time great wrestlers, amateur or professional, Henry Wittenberg won 400 consecutive matches—from the 1939 National Collegiate Athletic Association (NCAA) Championships to the 1952 Olympic Games in Helsinki.

During this time, Wittenberg won the Olympic Freestyle Light-Heavyweight gold medal in 1948, and a silver medal in the same weight at the 1952 Olympiad; and won the United States Amateur Athletic Union (AAU) Freestyle title eight times between 1940 and 1952—174-pound crowns in 1940 and 1941, and 191-pound titles in 1943, 1944, 1946, 1947, 1948, and 1952. He also captured gold medals as a Freestyle Heavyweight at both the 1950 and 1953 Maccabiah Games.

Wittenberg was captain of the 1952 United States Olympic Wrestling Team and coach of the first National (U.S.A.) team to compete in the Soviet Union (1959). He coached the U.S.A. wrestling team at the 1968 Olympic Games in Mexico, was wrestling coach at Yeshiva University (New York) from 1959 to 1967, and coached at City College of New York (CCNY) from 1967 to 1979.

He is a member of the National Wrestling Hall of Fame.

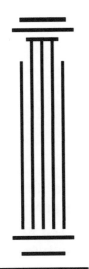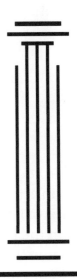

YACHTING

ZEFANIA CARMEL and LYDIA LAZAROV
Israel
Carmel—Born December 21, 1940, in Baghdad, Iraq
Died September 1980

Lazarov—Born January 16, 1946, in Sofia, Bulgaria

Israel's first World Champions in any sport, Zefania Carmel and Lydia Lazarov won that first World title in 1969, at Sandham, Sweden, in the Team 420 Non-Olympic Sailing Class. At the same competition, Carmel also won the World Championship in the Individual event.

As teammates on Israel's Zevulun Bateam Club, they won the Israeli National Championship in 1966 in the 420-Class, and finished ahead of an international field of competition in the same event in August 1967, on New York's Hudson River. Carmel won the Israel National Individual event in 1970.

Carmel drowned in September 1980, while training on a windsurfing craft.

WALENTIN MANKIN
Soviet Union
Born August 19, 1938

Mankin is the only yachtsman to win Olympic gold medals in three different classes of boats, in three Olympiads. He won his first gold in 1968 at Mexico City in the Finn Class, 11.7 points. His second was won at the 1972 Munich Games in the Tempest Class (with Dyrdyra), 28.1 points. And he captured his third gold medal in the Star Class (with Muzyschenko), 24.7 points, at the 1980 Moscow Olympics. Mankin also took an Olympic silver medal in the Tempest Class at the 1976 Montreal Games.

THE PILLAR OF ACHIEVEMENT

The Pillar of Achievement recognizes Jewish men and women who have made significant contributions to sports, as well as significant contributions to society through sports.

JEHOSHUA ALOUF (Wolpiansky)
Israel

Jehoshua Alouf organized the first five World Maccabiah Games and was one of the founders of the Israel Sports Federation. A pioneer in physical education and sports in the Holy Land, Alouf, in 1935, became Supervisor of Physical Education in Palestine, and served as Director of the Israel Department of Physical Education, 1953–1957. He settled in Palestine in 1912, from Slonim, Russia.

DR. ROBERT ATLASZ
Germany & Israel

Robert Atlasz was a leader of the German Maccabi movement during the rise of Nazism in the mid-1930s. He settled in Palestine in 1937, serving the Maccabi World Union as its Chairman of Track and Field, 1937–1952, and Sports Director, 1939–1965. Dr. Atlasz, a dentist, was in charge of sports for the World Maccabiah Games of 1950, 1953, 1957, and 1961. He has been a member of the Israel Olympic Committee since 1959.

BARUCH BAGG
Israel

General Secretary of the Palestine/Israel Physical Training Department, 1939–1953, Baruch Bagg was instrumental in the establishment of the Wingate Institute for Physical Education (Israel) in 1957, and was a director of the Institute. He was secretary of Hapoel, 1932–1933. He first settled in Palestine in 1929, from Riga, Latvia.

MORRIS "MOE" BERG
United States

A Major League Baseball catcher and shortstop with five teams, 1923–1939, Moe Berg was a solid, albeit journeyman, player with a lifetime batting average of .243, a Princeton University degree, and the ability to speak in 12 languages (including Japanese, Spanish, Latin, and Portuguese).

It was the language credentials, combined with his baseball persona, that motivated the U.S. Government in 1942 to convince Berg to leave his coaching job with the Boston Red Sox and undertake a still-secret mission (several books call it spying) in South America. He subsequently broadcast to the Japanese during World War II for the United States, and became a counter-intelligence agent in Europe. Without commenting on the specifics of Berg's government assignments, officials have referred to him as "a hero," and described the results of his efforts as "invaluable to our country."

It was Berg the athlete that inspired a baseball scout in 1922 to coin the classic remark: "Good field, no hit." Berg played for the Brooklyn Dodgers (1923), Chicago White Sox (1926–1930), Cleveland Indians (1931 and 1934), Washington Senators (1932 and 1934), Boston Red Sox (1935–1939), and was a Red Sox coach until 1942. He died in May 1972.

GRETEL BERGMANN
Germany

As Germany's leading female high-jumper during the 1930s, Gretel Bergmann was one of two Jews named to the German Olympic team for the 1936 Berlin Olympiad. However, only weeks prior to those Games, when an international movement to boycott the Nazi-influenced Olympiad had subsided, she was declared unqualified to compete by the German Olympic Committee.

Bergmann (today Mrs. Margaret Lambert) was elected to the Pillar as a representative of all Jewish athletes—including 21 other German-Jewish Olympic candidates—who were not permitted by national policies to compete in the 1936 Olympics.

DR. RICHARD BLUM
Israel

In 1903, Richard Blum was one of the founding fathers of the Jüdische Turnerschaft, an umbrella organization for Jewish gymnastics clubs in Germany. The Turnerschaft was the forerunner of the Maccabi World Union.

HASKELL COHEN
United States

Haskell Cohen was Public Relations Director for the National Basketball Association (NBA), 1950–1969. He created the first NBA East-West All Star Game, and structured the first NBA college draft. He currently is a member of the Basketball Hall of Fame Board of Trustees, a member of the United States Olympic Basketball Committee, and a member of the Amateur Basketball Association USA, representing the National Jewish Welfare Board. Cohen was President, 1965–1975, of the United States Committee Sports for Israel, and was a member of that organization almost from its inception. He is the first non-Israeli to receive the Israel Olympic Medal, and has been the U.S. chairman of the Hapoel Games in Israel. He served, 1981–1989, as the first chairman of the International Jewish Sports Hall of Fame Selection Committee.

Cohen held the post of Sports Editor for the Jewish Telegraph Agency (JTA) for 17 years. As a longtime contributing sports editor to America's *Parade* magazine Sunday newspaper supplement, he originated the National Association of College Basketball Coaches All-America Team as well as the High School All-America Team.

MASSIMO DELLA PERGOLA
Italy

Massimo Della Pergola was Secretary-General of the International Sports Press Association, 1977–1988, and since 1989 has been the organization's Vice-President. As Italy's premier sports journalist, he has contributed to more than 65 newspapers and periodicals, and to Italian and international radio, television, and press agencies. Della Pergola has reported eleven Summer Olympic Games, three Winter Olympics, and eleven Soccer World Cups.

In 1946, as editor-in-chief of the Milan newspaper *Gazzetta dello Sport,* he founded the organization that launched Totocalcio, the football (soccer) pools system, to finance Italy's national soccer program and the Italian Olympic Committee. He is also founder of the Italian Sporting Press Union, and has served or currently serves in a variety of capacities in the Italian and world sports community.

Massimo is a "Grande Officiale" of the Republic of Italy, recipient of the Prize of the International Universities Sports Federation (he coined the name "Universiades" for the World University Championships), been presented the City of Milan gold medal, and received numerous other honors.

Since 1960, Massimo has been President of the Italian Maccabi Federation, and, 1961–1989, has been the responsible organizer of every Italian Maccabi Team competing in the World Maccabiah Games in Israel.

JUDITH DEUTSCH
Austria

An Austrian champion and record holder in freestyle swimming, 1933–1935, Judith Deutch was elected outstanding Austrian female athlete of 1935 and selected to represent her country in the 1936 Berlin Olympic Games. She refused to do so in protest against the policies of Nazi Germany. Suspended from competition by Austrian authorities, she emigrated to Palestine, and represented the Holy Land from then on. Deutsch was elected to the Pillar as a representative of the many athletes, worldwide, who had the opportunity to compete in the 1936 Olympiad but refused to do so in protest over German policies toward Jews and other minorities.

NAT FLEISCHER
United States

One of the founders of *Ring* magazine—the boxing "bible"—in 1922, Nat Fleischer was considered the world's most influential boxing authority until his death in 1972. He acquired sole ownership of the monthly *The Ring* in 1929, and devoted his life to it and to boxing.

A sportswriter for several New York City newspapers prior to his *Ring* magazine association, Fleischer wrote more than 40-million words on boxing during his career, including 57 books. He is one of the founders of the Boxing Hall of Fame and Museum. During his career, Fleischer not only refereed and judged more than 1,000 fights, but also participated in the awarding of championship belts and assisted in establishing boxing commissions throughout the world.

IAN FROMAN
South Africa

Ian Froman is one of four founding members of the Israel Tennis Centers and ITC's country-wide (Israel) program. A dentist who made *aliyah* (emigrated to Israel) in 1969, Froman has devoted his full time to the origination and development of the Israel Tennis Centers. While others, including American Pillar honoree Harold Landesberg (and William Lippy and Joseph Shane), are credited with providing the funds to create and maintain the ITC, it is Froman who accepted the hands-on responsibility for the program's conceptualization and development.

HARRY L. GETZ
South Africa

For many years, Harry Getz was a prominent official with the International Swimming Federation (FINA), and was one of the world's leading authorities on the sport of water polo.

PIERRE GILDESGAME
Great Britain

Pierre Gildesgame was the first Chairman of the Maccabi World Union. Under his leadership, the International Maccabiah Games Committee was founded in 1963, to serve as the organization responsible for overall supervision of the quadrennial World Maccabiah Games. Born in Poland, young Gildesgame and his older brother Leon walked from Galicia to Palestine, Pierre eventually emigrating to Great Britain and Leon to the United States. Gildesgame died in an auto accident in 1982.

EMMANUEL GILL
Israel

Emmanuel Gill was Sports Director of the Hapoel Sport Association for 35 years. He was Chairman of the Israel Sports Federation, 1967–1971, and a member of the Israel Olympic Committee. He is also author of a number of important books on sports.

CHAIM GLOVINSKY
Israel

Chaim Glovinsky headed Israel's first Olympic team in 1952, and again in 1956 and 1964. He served as Treasurer of the Israel Olympic Committee from 1952 until his death in 1986. Glovinsky was also Chairman of the Israel Sports Federation, 1961–1963, Chairman of Basketball in Israel from 1963 until his death, and President of the Israel Soccer Football Federation, 1938–1954. Born in Poland, Glovinsky settled in Palestine in 1920 and, in 1927, became one of the first members of Hapoel.

LESTER HARRISON
United States

A pioneer in American professional basketball as a player, coach, and team owner, Lester Harrison is one of the founders of the National Basketball Association (NBA), and was elected to the Basketball Hall of Fame in 1979. Having organized traveling semi-pro teams as early as the 1920s, Harrison formed the Rochester Pros in 1944 in his hometown, Rochester, New York. The following year, the Pros became the Rochester Royals when Harrison purchased a franchise in the National Basketball League. In 1946, the NBL merged into the Basketball Association of America, and in 1949 Harrison's Royals joined with seven other teams to form the National Basketball Association. With Harrison as owner-coach, the Royals won League Championships in 1946, 1947, and 1951. (His original franchise is now the Sacramento Kings.)

There was little media fanfare in 1946 when Harrison signed Dolly King to play for his NBL Royals, at the same time persuading the rival Buffalo Bisons team owner to sign player William "Pop" Gates. A year before Jackie Robinson integrated Major League baseball, King and Gates became the first blacks to play organized professional basketball.

GLADYS HELDMAN
United States

Gladys Heldman has been a prime mover in the stimulation and development of American tennis through the pages of *World Tennis* magazine, of which she is founder, editor, and publisher. The magazine first appeared in 1953, having been published originally for five years under the name *Houston Tennis*.

Heldman was a key organizer of the Virginia Slims Tennis Circuit, the first all-women's tennis tour. Rushing in "where wise men feared to tread," Heldman underwrote the 1959 National (USA) Indoor Championships when the United States Lawn Tennis Association decided that such an undertaking for the USLTA was financially unsound.

The entire Heldman family—husband Julius, and daughters Julie and Carrie—have played a prominent role in American tennis. Daughter Julie, was ranked number 2 in the United States in 1968 and 1969, number 5 World in 1969, and won the Maccabiah Games Singles, Doubles (with Marilyn Aschner), and Mixed Doubles (with Ed Rubinoff) in 1969. Gladys, herself, was ranked number 1 in the State of Texas and number 2 in the Southwest in 1954, and that year played in the early rounds at Wimbledon.

COL. HARRY D. HENSHEL
United States

A founder of the United States Committee Sports for Israel in 1948, Harry D. Henshel served as the organization's first president. He was a member of the U.S. Olympic Basketball Committee from its inception in 1936 until his death in 1961, serving as its chairman in 1956.

Henshel is the father of Harry B. Henshel, longtime American track official and developer in 1948 of the Bulova Phototimer, the first sports automatic timing device. (Harry B. was President of the Bulova Watch Company, and father Harry D. was Bulova's Vice-president.) Henshel *père* was a major influence on and benefactor of American Jewish charitable organizations and projects.

JOSEPH INBAR (Burstein)
Israel

Joseph Inbar was Co-Chairman of the Israel Olympic Committee from 1963 until 1980. He was a member of the Executive Committee of Hapoel, 1938–1982, and its General Secretary beginning in 1962. He also served as Chairman of Israel Basketball, 1956–1962, and Chairman of the Israel Soccer Football Federation, 1958–1959.

MAX KASE
United States

The longtime sports editor of the *New York Journal American* newspaper, Max Kase was one of the founders of the influential B'nai B'rith Sports Lodge of New York City, serving two terms as its president. In 1957, Kase was instrumental in arranging Hearst Newspapers' underwriting and promotion of the Israel National Basketball Team's first visit to the United States.

HAROLD LANDESBERG
United States

One of the founders and prime mover of the Israel Tennis Centers in Ramat Hasharon and throughout Israel (with Rubin Josephs, Dr. William Lippy, and Joseph Shane), Harold Landesberg was the first Chairman of the ITC Committee, and first President of the ITC Association.

DR. HERMAN LELLEWER
Germany

Dr. Herman Lellewer was the dynamic leader of the Maccabi World Union, 1927–1935, when the movement's world headquarters were in Berlin, Germany. He spearheaded Maccabi's resisitance to Nazism until 1935, when the movement moved its chief offices to London. It was under Dr. Lellewer's leadership that the first World Maccabiah Games were held in Palestine in the spring of 1932.

WILLY MEISL
Germany

Willy Meisl was Germany's leading sportswriter from 1920 through the mid-1930s, when he was forced by the Nazis to flee to England. Meisl also coached swimming and soccer in Sweden, and has authored numerous books on both sports. He is the brother of Hugo Meisel, Austrian soccer mentor and honoree in the IJSHOF.

BARNEY NAGLER
United States

For nearly 40 years, Barney Nagler wrote a newspaper column devoted mainly to boxing and thoroughbred racing. The column, "On Second Thought," first appeared in 1950 in the *New York Morning Telegraph,* and was spiced with jargon of the gym and stable. When the *Telegraph* ceased publication in 1972, Nagler's column moved to the *Daily Racing Form,* continuing until the writer's death in October 1990. Nagler served as President of the New York Boxing Writers Association twelve times between 1960 and 1980, and from 1984 to 1989 he was president of the Boxing Writers Association of America—from which he received the James A. Farley Award in the latter year. In 1978, Nagler was honored with the Walter Haight Award by the National Turf Writers Association for excellence in reporting thoroughbred racing. An author of many books, Nagler's titles include: *James Norris and the Decline of Boxing, The American Horse, Brown Bomber: The Pilgrimage of Joe Louis, Only the Ring Was Square* (with Teddy Brenner), and *Shoemaker, America's Greatest Jockey.*

FRED OBERLANDER
Canada

In 1949, Fred Oberlander founded the Canadian Maccabi Association. In 1930, as a youth, the Austrian-born wrestler won the Austrian Heavyweight Championship—followed by eight French championships, 1931–1938, the European Heavyweight title in 1935, eight British

CHARLES ORENSTEIN
United States

One of the leading figures in the amateur sports movement within the United States for more than 40 years, Charles Orenstein was a member of the United States Olympic Committee from 1924 until his death in 1966. Orenstein was chief spokesman for the Jewish community on all matters concerning amateur athletics. During his early years on the USOC, he was the representative of the U.S. Army, and for nearly four decades represented the Jewish Welfare Board on the Committee.

Orenstein was a member of the Executive Committee of both the Amateur Athletic Union (AAU) and USOC; and, in 1948, was named Chairman of the United States Olympic Food and Housing Committee, with responsibility for providing housing and food for all American athletes participating in the Olympic Games. His reputation as a provider had spread so, that at the 1964 Tokyo Olympics, he also fed the Canadian and British athletes—in all, more than 1,000 Olympians daily.

As Chairman of the Jewish Welfare Board's national Health and Physical Education Committee from its inception in 1943 until his death in September 1966, Orenstein played a leading role in the creation and expansion of sports and recreational activities at Jewish Community Centers and YM-YWHAs throughout the world.

With AAU President Jeremiah T. Mahoney, Orenstein played a major role in dramatic, but unsuccessful, efforts to have the United States boycott the 1936 Berlin Olympics. Orenstein was one of the four founders (with Harry Henshel, Edward Rosenblum, and Harold Zimman) of the United States Committee Sports for Israel in May 1948. In 1950, he and the Committee were key figures in helping Israel obtain membership on the International Olympic Committee.

BERNARD POSTAL
United States

Bernard Postal is co-author (with Jesse and Roy Silver) of the *Encyclopedia of Jews in Sports*, the extensive 526-page reference "bible" on Jewish athletes and sportsmen, published in 1965 (Bloch). While the *Encyclopedia* was a labor of love, Postal was also full-time editor of the Seven Arts Feature Syndicate, distributor of news to Anglo-Jewish newspapers in the United States and worldwide.

SHIRLEY POVICH
United States

Shirley Povich has been a sports reporter and columnist for the *Washington* (DC) *Post* for 68 years. In 1976, he was one of the first members of the media to be presented with the Ford Frick Award, on his election to Major League Baseball's Hall of Fame. Among the many honors he has received are the Grantland Rice Sportswriting Award in 1964 and election to the National Sportswriters Hall of Fame in 1984. Povich, the father of American television personality Maury Povich, was also listed in *Who's Who in American Women* in 1962!

DANIEL PRENN
Germany & Great Britain

Daniel Prenn was called "Europe's number one man" by *American Lawn Tennis* magazine in 1932, following Davis Cup triumphs over Britain's top seeds Fred Perry and Bunny Austin and America's Frank Shields. In the World Top Ten rankings, Prenn was number 8 in 1929 (Bill Tilden), number 6 in 1932 (England's A. Wallis Myers), and number 7 in 1934 *(American Lawn Tennis)*. Prenn was at the top of his game, ranked number 1 for Germany four straight years (1928–1932), when he was barred from competition as the Nazis came to power in 1933.

The German Tennis Federation passed these resolutions (in part) in April 1933: "No Jew may be selected for a national team or the Davis Cup. No Jewish or Marxist club or association may be affiliated with the German Tennis Federation. The player Dr. Prenn (a Jew) will not be selected for the Davis Cup team in 1933."

Prenn moved to England soon afterwards, but while he continued to play, he never quite recaptured the level of tennis he had reached in Germany.

FRED SCHMERTZ
United States

Fred Schmertz was one of the founders of the Millrose Athletic Association in 1908 in New York City. In 1915, he became Assistant Director of the Millrose Games—known in the United States as the "Indoor Olympics"—and served in that capacity until 1933, when he became Meet Director. He held that post until 1974, retiring at age 85. Schmertz served in an official capacity with several U.S.A. Olympic teams dating back to 1928. In 1961, he was Chairman of the United States Maccabiah track team.

ERIC SEELIG
Germany

Twenty-three-year-old Eric Seelig was Germany's Middleweight and Light-Heavyweight boxing champion in 1933, when Hitler came to power. On a July evening that year, the night that Seelig was scheduled to defend his Middleweight title in Berlin, Nazi goons threatened him with death if he entered the ring. Seelig fled to France that night, competing there for several years before emigrating to the United States via Cuba in 1935. While in France, he fought two Middleweight title bouts against World Champion Marcel Thil, both ending unsuccessfully by decision.

A punishing battler, Seelig enjoyed considerable success in the United States, finishing his career with 40 bouts (11 KOs), 7 draws, and 8 losses. His highest *Ring* magazine ranking was 6th, in 1938. To this day, Germany has not restored recognition of his stripped titles.

EMMANUEL SIMON
Israel

Emmanuel Simon was a pioneer in sports medicine, and beginning in 1924, one of the pioneers of physical education and sports in Palestine. Simon was the first Director of the Israeli governmental body responsible for sports, 1948–1953. He died in May 1989.

DR. URIEL SIMRI
Israel

The first Director of the International Jewish Sports Hall of Fame, Dr. Uriel Simri is recognized as one of the world's leading authorities and educators on physical culture. A prominent author, international lecturer, and governmental advisor, he is Past-President of the Society of the History of Physical Education and Sport in Asia, and Secretary/ Treasurer of the International Society for Comparative Physical Education and Sport.

Since 1966, Dr. Simri has been associated with the Wingate Institute of Physical Education and Sport in Israel—the only physical education campus in the Middle East. He has held various key positions at Wingate, including Deputy Director and Scientific Director. An international basketball (FIBA) referee, 1954–1961, Simri was the first Israeli ever selected to officiate Olympic Games competition—as a basketball referee at the 1956 Melbourne Games.

OSCAR STATE
Great Britain

Secretary of the International Weightlifting Federation, 1960–1974, Oscar State managed and coached British and Empire lifters for the 1948 Olympics and for the 1950 and 1958 Empire Games. He served as Secretary of the British Weightlifting Association, 1946–1950, and Secretary of the British Empire and Commonwealth Weightlifting Committee, 1948–1972. State organized Olympic weightlifting in Great Britain in 1948 and 1956, as well as many World Championships and Empire Games.

LEWIS STEIN
United States

New York tenpin bowling champion Lewis Stein attended a meeting of the New York Bowlers Association on September 9, 1895, that laid the foundation for what was to become the American Bowling Congress. At that meeting, Stein proposed that bowling be scored on a

300-point system—instead of the then-popular 200-point basis—and that 16 pounds be the maximum legal weight of a bowling ball. Both proposals were accepted, and remain in effect, worldwide, to this day. At the time of his death in October 1949, Stein was the last surviving charter member of the American Bowling Congress.

ARTHUR TAKAC
Hungary

Arthur Takac was advisor to the Program Committee of the International Olympic Committee for many years, and one of the established international authorities in the field of sports.

BEN WEIDER
Canada

Ben Weider is President of the International Federation of Bodybuilders. He and brother Joe Weider founded the IFBB in 1946, in Montreal, Canada, in order to unify, control, and coordinate the sport of bodybuilding throughout the world. As a member of the General Association of International Sports Federations since 1969, Weider's IFBB represents 134 countries in the area of physical culture and bodybuilding. Among its many activities, the IFBB provides research to national Olympic Committees, international sports federations, and the International Federation of Sports Medicine. Since 1946, the World Amateur Bodybuilding Championships have been sanctioned by the IFBB. In support of youth fitness programs and sports research throughout the world, Weider has contributed state-of-the-art training gymnasia to many countries, including Germany, Syria, Lebanon, Israel, the People's Republic of China, Canada, and the United States.

Honored throughout the world for his dedicated service, Weider is a recipient of the Order of Canada, and was a nominee for the Nobel Peace Prize in 1984.

JOE WEIDER
United States

Since 1939, Joe Weider has been the primary force in advancing the sport of bodybuilding throughout the world via magazine publications, sponsorship of physical development contests—including the Mr. and Mrs. Olympia Contest—and the development, manufacture, and distribution of nutritional and exercise equipment products. In 1939, seven years before he and his brother Ben founded the International Federation of Bodybuilders, Joe published the first issue of *Your Physique* magazine. In 1968, *YP* became *Muscle & Fitness,* and today it is the flagship of the Weider Health and Fitness Company publishing empire. Other Weider-published magazines are: *Shape, Men's Fitness,* and *Flex.* A vast variety of Weider-manufactured nutritional aides and exercise equipment is distributed throughout the world.

CHAIM WEIN
Israel

One of Israel's sports pioneers, Chaim Wein was a founder of the Palestine/Israel Sports Federation in 1931, and served as its Co-Chairman, 1957–1963. Wein was Chairman of the Sports Committee of Maccabi, 1944–1962, Director of the Physical Education Teachers College, 1944–1960, and Supervisor of Physical Education in Israel, 1960–1981. He emigrated to Palestine in 1921 from Russia.

JOSEPH YEKUTIELI
Israel

The lone delegate from Palestine to the 1929 World Maccabi Congress, Joseph Yekutieli presented a concept for what he called the Maccabiah Games. The proposal was unanimously approved and the first Maccabiah took place in Tel Aviv, March 29 to April 6, 1932.

AVIEZER YELLIN
Israel

Aviezer Yellin founded the first gymnastics club in Palestine in 1906, the first Maccabi Club in Jerusalem in 1911, and the National Maccabi Association in Palestine in 1912.

HAROLD O. ZIMMAN
United States

Publisher of *The Olympian,* the official magazine of the United States Olympic Committee, Harold O. Zimman has served as a member of the USOC since 1952, and for many years has sat on the Committee's executive board. Since 1948, he has been a member of the Board of Directors of the Jewish Welfare Board, and has served as Chairman of its Health and Physical Education Committee since 1958. In 1966, Zimman was appointed by the JWB to serve on the USOC as spokesman for the American Jewish community.

In 1948, Zimman and three others (Charles Ornstein, Harry D. Henshel, and Edward Rosenblum) founded the United States Committee Sports for Israel, with the vision of helping Israel obtain membership in the International Olympic community. Goal accomplished—Israel competed in the 1952 Games—Zimman remains active in the USCSFI's numerous other U.S.–Israel sports-related projects, including the World Maccabiah Games. He has also been a prime mover in the development of sports facilities in the United States and in Israel.

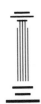

APPENDIX:
"THE PARTNERSHIP"

The International Jewish Sports Hall of Fame is a "partnership" between the United States Committee Sports for Israel, the Wingate Institute of Physical Education and Sport, some of the world's leading sports authorities, and interested, active, and generous Jews.

THE INTERNATIONAL JEWISH SPORTS HALL OF FAME

The International Jewish Sports Hall of Fame/Yad Le'ish Hasport Hayehudi was formally inaugurated on July 7, 1981. Its predecessor, the Jewish Sports Hall of Fame, was founded in the United States in May 1979. The original Hall of Fame included only American honorees. The International Hall of Fame honors athletes and sportsmen throughout the world.

The purpose of the IJSHOF is to honor Jewish men and women, world-wide, who have accomplished extraordinary achievements in sports and to recognize other Jewish men and women who have made significant contributions to society through sports.

The IJSHOF is governed by its International Executive Board (IEB), each of its members elected to four-year terms. The guiding principle of the IJSHOF is: "The Deeds of the Past Shall Inspire the Achievements of the Future."

Elections to the Hall of Fame are conducted by the International Selection Committee (ISC). Members of the ISC are appointed to that post by the IEB. Names of ISC members are not publicly disclosed (other than the sitting chairman), but each individual serving on the ISC is an international or national authority (in his/her country) on sports past and/or present. They operate as an autonomous group, and as such the ISC considers all nominations independently of the IEB (and any other body), delivering its final decisions based upon its own determinations. In matters relating to the Pillar of Achievement, however, the ISC nominates candidates to the Pillar whose names are submitted to the IEB for final approval.

There are two basic categories of honorees within the IJSHOF: (1) those elected for athletic excellence, and other special instances—the ISC determines situations of "special instances"—and (2) those elected to the Pillar of Achievement for specific contributions to sports and/or society via sports.

The inaugural honorees of the original Jewish Sports Hall of Fame, the opening ceremonies of which were celebrated in a dinner at the Los Angeles Beverly Hilton Hotel on May 20, 1979. They include (left to right): Nat Holman, Red Auerbach, Dolph Schayes, Sylvia Wene Martin, Hank Greenberg, Warren Abrams (Maccabiah Games chairman), Dick Savitt, Jackie Fields, Jim Jacobs, and Irving Jaffee. Of the attending inductees, only Sid Luckman is missing from this photograph.

Elections to the IJSHOF are made annually, with no more than ten honorees named in any calendar year. Announcements of each election are made on/or about December 1 for the succeeding year.

Anyone can submit nominations to the IJSHOF. These should be made to the Executive Director, Wingate Institute, Wingate Post Office, 42902 Netanya, Israel. All submissions of nominations should be accompanied by as much support information on the candidate(s) as is available.

Israeli sports leaders and executives of the United States Committee Sports for Israel are all smiles following the signing of the Israel Charter for the new International Jewish Sports Hall of Fame. Standing (left to right): Joseph Siegman, international chairman of the IJSHOF; Haim Glovinsky, executive director and treasurer, Israel Olympic Committee; Haskell Cohen, chairman, IJSHOF Selection Committee; Dr. Uriel Simri, scientific director, Wingate Institute, and executive director, IJSHOF; Paul Ash, member IJSHOF Executive Committee; and Alan Sherman, chairman, IJSHOF Founders Committee, and chairman, IJSHOF Dedication Committee. Seated (left to right): Ziporah Seidner, public relations director, Wingate Institute; the Honorable Eliezer Shmueli, director general, Israel Ministry of Education and Culture, and IJSHOF honorary chairman; and Uri Afek, director, Israel Sports and Physical Education Authority.

UNITED STATES COMMITTEE SPORTS FOR ISRAEL

The International Jewish Sports Hall of Fame began as a fund raising project for the USCSFI in 1979. Sports For Israel was founded in May 1948, for the purpose of assisting the then new State of Israel in its efforts to enter the Olympic Games community. The four men who organized the group—Harry Henshel, Charles Orenstein, Edward Rosenblum, and Harold Zimman—stated as their purpose: "To help Israel develop its full potential as a nation, and enhance its quality of life through sports."

Enjoying success in its original endeavor—Israel competed in its first Olympiad in 1952—the USCSFI, in 1953, undertook the responsibility of organizing and sponsoring the United States team to the World Maccabiah Games. It has continued with this growing responsibility ever since.

Over the years, in addition to sponsorship of the quadrennial Maccabiah Games, the USCSFI has taken on numerous other activities to promote physical education and sports programs in Israel and within the United States. In 1957, the USCSFI helped found (and continues to support) the Wingate Institute for Physical Education and Sport in Netanya, the only university-level campus in the Middle East devoted to sports. The organization is a major supporter of the Ilan Sport Centre for the Physically Disabled in Ramat Gan, a non-residential therapeutic facility for physically disabled children and adults.

In the early 1980s, the USCSFI provided the primary funding for the Robert Feldman Sports Centre at the Kadoori Agricultural Training School in Lower Galilee; supported the Beit Halochem sports and rehabilitation social center for Israel's disabled war veterans and their families; supported the Israel Tennis Centers program since its inception (the ITC program began its development under the auspices of the USCSFI); is one of three sponsors/organizers of the North American Maccabi Youth Games held every other year; sponsors the U.S.A. Pan American Maccabiah Games Teams; and, since 1949, has sent top American coaches to the Holy Land to teach sports—the likes of Nat Holman (who introduced basketball to Israel in 1949), John Wooden, and Mark Spitz, among many others.

The USCSFI also provides financial aid to Israeli athletes and coaches, often in the form of scholarships to American universities; sends American youth teams to Israel, and brings Israeli teams to the U.S.; has arranged for professional NBA teams to play exhibitions in Israel; and sponsors participation in various activities within Jewish community programs throughout the world.

The Jewish Sports Hall of Fame was created in 1979 by USCSFI vice-president Joe Siegman, and nearly all of its primary funding is a result of the efforts of USCSFI vice-president Alan Sherman. Sports for Israel has earnestly supported the project from its inception. The Hall of Fame became International at the close of the USCSFI presidency of Nat Holman, just prior to the 11th Maccabiah Games. In the fall of 1981, under succeeding USCSFI president Bob Spivak, annual financial support to the international entity was initiated, as well as the services and advice of the USCSFI national staff and offices.

The USCSFI maintains its headquarters in Philadelphia, Pennsylvania, with regional offices in Los Angeles and Miami. While the organization employs a modest staff of professionals to coordinate and maintain the Committee's many on-going projects, nearly all of its vast network of officers, directors, coaches, and project leaders are volunteers.

Maccabiah athletes representing thirty-four countries parade through the streets of Old Jerusalem in the Games' traditional closing ceremonies at the Western Wall. The USCSFI sponsors and selects the United States Maccabiah Team.

THE WINGATE INSTITUTE

The Wingate Institute for Physical Education and Sport is home to the International Jewish Sports Hall of Fame. Wingate is Israel's National Center for physical education and sport.

The Institute was dedicated on April 7, 1957, named in honor of Major General Orde Charles Wingate, the British officer who played a leading role in both organizing Israel's pre-state underground army and supporting statehood for Israel.

Situated on 125 acres of verdant landscape near the town of Netanya, the institute overlooks the Mediterranean Sea. It lies approximately 20 miles north of Tel Aviv on the main Haifa-Tel Aviv highway.

Wingate serves as a training center for Israel's national teams competing in international events, including the Olympic Games. It also serves as a base for national and international professional conferences and seminars.

The campus comprises the following Schools, Departments, and amenities:

- Zinman College of Physical Education
- School of Physiotherapy
- Nat Holman School for Coaches and Instructors
- Sport Department (research, sport medicine, elite sport, and development)
- Instructional Media Department
- Handicapped and Senior programs
- 36-room hotel
- 3,000-seat open-air Amphitheater
- Residential dormitories
- Gymnasiums, sport fields, a stadium, outdoor and indoor courts, 50-meter swimming pool
- Dining rooms and cafeterias

The IJSHOF is located on the third floor of the Student Union Building—the grand foyer to the campus auditorium.

The Wingate Institute was dedicated on April 7, 1957, in honor of Major General Orde Charles Wingate (1903–1944), an ardent supporter of Jewish independence in Palestine during the British Mandate that followed World War I. Wingate, a thirty-three-year-old intelligence officer, arrived in Palestine in 1936, at a time when casualties from Arab attacks on Jewish settlements had reached alarming numbers. The then-British Army captain, a Christian, organized and trained Jewish settlers into "night squads" to combat the anti-Jewish violence. He would tell his trainees: "Our purpose here is to found the Jewish army!" The Jews of Palestine called him "Hayedid" (The Friend); the Wingate Institute is one of many entities within the State of Israel that are named in honor of "Hayedid."

DISTINGUISHED AUTHORITIES ON SPORTS

The International Jewish Sports Hall of Fame is fortunate to have had the knowledgable guidance of Dr. Uriel Simri as its first Executive Director. He is one of the world's foremost authorities on international sports and, without question, the leading world authority on Jews in sports. Professor, prolific author, international lecturer, and Wingate scientific and faculty leader, Dr. Simri served as curator of the IJSHOF through its first eight years.

The chairman of the International Selection Committee during its first eight years was Haskell Cohen. Cohen was Publicity Director for the National Basketball Association in its earliest years, 1950–69, and is a longtime member of the Basketball Hall of Fame Board of Trustees (the group that elects individuals into that Hall of Fame). For 17 years, Cohen served as Sports Editor for the Jewish Telegraph Agency (JTA), and he is a contributing sports editor to *Parade* magazine's Sunday newspaper supplement.

The Executive Director and ISC Chairman have received extensive support in gathering and evaluating information regarding candidates for election to the IJSHOF from the following distinguished sports authorities:

Robert Atlasz — a leader of the German Maccabi movement during the 1930s, who has served the Maccabi World Union in Palestine/Israel in various capacities since 1937, including sports chairman of the 1950, 1953, 1957, and 1961 Maccabiah Games. He has been a member of the Israel Olympic Committee since 1959.

Massimo Della Pergola — Secretary-General (1977–1988) and Vice-President (1989–present) of the International Sports Press Association. He is Italy's leading sportswriter.

George Eisen — internationally published author and lecturer on subjects relating to the history of sports and physical education. A member of the 1956 Hungarian Olympic boxing team, he later coached the national boxing team of Israel.

Kenneth J. Gradon — a prominent British sports official, active for nearly four decades in Maccabi World Union activities.

Arthur Hanak — Archivist of the Maccabi World Union, and curator of the Pierre Gildesgame Museum, Kfar Hamaccabiah, Ramat Gan, Israel.

Fred Oberlander — winner of the heavyweight wrestling championships of Austria, France, Great Britain, Europe, and Canada 19 times in 21 years (1930–51). A member of Hakoah-Vienna during his youth, he is the founder of the Canadian Maccabi Association.

Israel Paz — Sports Editor of *Ha'aretz,* Israel's leading Hebrew-language daily newspaper.

Bernard Postal — one of three authors of *The Encyclopedia of Jews in Sports.* The late Mr. Postal was also editor of the Seven Arts Feature Syndicate, distributor of news to Anglo-Jewish newspapers worldwide.

Jesse Silver — Sports Editor of the *Encyclopedia Judaica* and *Encyclopedia Judaica Yearbook,* and one of three authors of *The Encyclopedia of Jews in Sports.*

Roy Silver — one of three authors of *The Encyclopedia of Jews in Sports,* and a sports writer/producer for the NBC and ABC television networks for many years. He was one of the first consultants to the original Jewish Sports Hall of Fame.

Robert Slater — author of *Great Jews in Sports* and four novels. A *Time* magazine reporter since 1976, headquartered in their Jerusalem bureau, he was chairman of the Foreign Press Association in 1987.

Shel Wallman — columnist-reporter for *Jewish Post* News Service and widely read in American-Jewish newspapers and periodicals.

Elli Wohlgelernter — Managing Editor of the Jewish Telegraphic Agency, New York, and longtime reporter-editor for Anglo and Jewish newspapers and the broadcast media.

THE ACTIVE AND THE GENEROUS

Many individuals have contributed to the International Jewish Sports Hall of Fame—some with energy and involvement, some with currency, many with both. Little could have been accomplished during the first decade of the IJSHOF without the contributions of those listed below.

Those who have served as members of the International Executive Board (IEB), 1981–93:

URI AFEK ...	Director General of the Olympic Committee of Israel
MICHAEL ALMOG ...	General Secretary of the Union of Local Authorities in Israel
PAUL ASH ...	USCSFI—Tucson, Arizona
SIMON ATLAS ...	USCSFI—Philadelphia, Pennsylvania
RICHARD BATCHLEY ...	USCSFI—Canoga Park, California
JEROME BLOOMBERG ...	USCSFI—Fort Lee, New Jersey
ZEEV BRAVERMAN ...	General Secretary of Elitzur-Israel
RAY BRENNER ...	USCSFI—New York City
ITZCHAK CASPI ...	Chairman of Maccabi Israel and Honorary Secretary of the Israel Olympic Committee
ALLAN DALFEN ...	USCSFI—Beverly Hills, California
AHARON DORON ...	Major General (ret.), Israel Defense Forces
SIMON DENNENBERG ...	USCSFI—Philadelphia, Pennsylvania
ALEX FISHER ...	Chairman, Maccabi-Canada
YAIR FRISHMAN ...	Deputy Director of the Sport and Physical Education Authority—State of Israel
HARRY GLICKMAN ...	USCSFI—Portland, Oregon
CHAIM GLOVINSKY ...	Leader of Israel's first Olympic teams and Treasurer of the Israel Olympic Committee
SIDNEY GREENBERG ...	Canadian Maccabiah Games Chairman
YIG'AL GRIFFEL ...	Chairman of Betar—Israel
ADY GROSS-PRYWES ...	Editor of bi-monthly *Hachinuch Hagufani ve'Hasport*—Israel
BARRY GURLAND ...	USCSFI—Miami, Florida

ALAN HAHN . . . USCSFI—Los Angeles, California

ARYEH HALEVI . . . Director of the Wingate Institute

JOSEPH INBAR . . . Treasurer and Past-President of the Israel Olympic Committee

HERB KUPERSMITH . . . USCSFI—Philadelphia, Pennsylvania

JEFFREY LAIKIND . . . USCSFI—New York City

JOSEPH MERBACK . . . USCSFI—Los Angeles, California

AZRIKAM MILCHAN . . . Vice-President, Israel Olympic Committee

MELVYN MILLER . . . USCSFI—Philadelphia, Pennsylvania

ARNOLD NELSON . . . USCSFI—Beverly Hills, California

ISAAC OFEK . . . President of Israel Olympic Committee and General Secretary of Hapoel

YARIV OREN . . . Deputy Director General of the Israel Ministry of Education and Culture, and Director of the Sport and Physical Education Authority of Israel

FRED SCHOENFELD . . . USCSFI—New York City

ZIPORA SEIDNER . . . Director of Public Relations, Wingate Institute

ALAN SHERMAN . . . USCSFI—Bethesda, Maryland

ELIEZER SHMUELI . . . Managing Director, Beth Hatefusoth Museum, Tel Aviv University

SHELDON SIDLOW . . . USCSFI—Sherman Oaks, California

JOSEPH SIEGMAN . . . USCSFI—Beverly Hills, California

DR. URIEL SIMRI . . . Chairman of Department for Social Sciences—Zinman College, Wingate

ROBERT E. SPIVAK . . . President, USCSFI—Philadelphia, Pennsylvania

WILLIAM STEERMAN . . . USCSFI—Philadelphia, Pennsylvania

GARY ULRICH . . . Chairman, Maccabi-Canada

CHAIM WEIN . . . Chairman of Israel Sports Federation, and Director of Israel's Physical Education Teachers' College

GILAD WEINGARTEN . . . Director, Wingate Institute
FRED WORMS . . . Chairman, Maccabi-Great Britain, and
President Maccabi World Union
MICHAEL WRUBELSKY . . . Chairman, Maccabi-Australia
HAROLD O. ZIMMAN . . . USCSFI—Boston

THE GENEROUS

The following dedications were made through the generosity of those indicated:

Pillar of Faith — a memorial to the Eleven Israeli Munich Olympic Games murder victims; dedicated by the Bender Foundation, Washington, D.C.

Pillar of Achievement — an honor roll of outstanding contributions to sports and society through sports; dedicated by Harry, Dorothy, Neil B., Debbie, and Denise Blumenthal, San Francisco, and by Richard S., Carole R., Stuart, Dennis, and Cindy Shostak, Encino, California.

Display Case — the Sherman Families: Ernest, Charles, Alan, and Neil, Washington, D.C.

Display Case — in honor of Harold Landesberg, 1982 Sportsman of the Year; dedicated by the United States Committee Sports for Israel, Philadelphia, Pennsylvania.

Piero Brolis Sculpture — dedicated to the eleven Israeli Olympians slain at the 1972 Games in Munich, Germany; sculptor Piero Brolis (Bergamo, Italy/1920–78); donated by his widow and family in 1982.

Ziva Lieblich Sculpture — sculptor Ziva Lieblich, Tel Aviv, Israel; made by Y. Dalva Studio, Y. Sharon; donated in 1981 by the Jerry Oren Family, Beverly Hills, California, in memory of Ahuva and Reuven Lavitz.

Maurice Podoloff Window — stained-glass window that was a permanent exhibit in the original Basketball Hall of Fame, Springfield Massachusetts; donated by the Basketball Hall of Fame, through the efforts of Haskell Cohen.

TRIBUTES

The generosity of the following individuals is expressed in special "Tributes" to specified honorees. The names of the Tribute donor appears on the display case of the tributed Hall of Fame member:

MEL ALLEN — Ralph J. Shapiro Family, Los Angeles, California
ARNOLD "RED" AUERBACH — Harold Butler Family, U.S.A.
ANGELA BUXTON — Fred Worms, London, England
EDDIE GOTTLIEB — Melvin K. Miller Family, Philadelphia, Pennsylvania
SANDY KOUFAX — Bender Foundation, Washington, D.C.
BENNY LEONARD — Harry and Dorothy Blumenthal, San Francisco
HARRY LITWACK — Martin Olinsky, Philadelphia, Pennsylvania
BARNEY ROSS — Faye and Ben Manger, Stamford, Connecticut
ADOLPH SCHAYES — Terry L. Cole Family, Ventura, California

THE FOUNDERS

The following individuals, families, organizations, and companies, contributed to the development and reality of the International Jewish Sports Hall of Fame. They are the Founders:

Bobbie and Warren Abrams, New York City
The Artery Organization, Inc., Chevy Chase, Maryland
Mr. and Mrs. Paul Ash, Tucson, Arizona
Mr. and Mrs. Leonard J. Attman, Glen Burnie, Maryland
Anne and Hy Barry, Beverly Hills, California
Mr. and Mrs. Howard Bender, Bethesda, Maryland
Dr. and Mrs. Benjamin Berger, Shaker Heights, Ohio
    — in memory of David Mark Berger
Mr. Charles Berman, Philadelphia, Pennsylvania
Dorothy and David "Bud" Block, Richmond, Virginia
Harriet and Cy Block, Lake Success, New York
May and Bernard Blumenthal, Brooklyn, New York
Mr. and Mrs. Harry Blumenthal, Santa Rosa, California

Mr. and Mrs. Neil Blumenthal, San Francisco, California
Shirley and Sol Bodner, Brooklyn, New York
Dr. Jerome L. Bornstein, Encino, California
Ruth and Ray Raymond B. Brenner, New York City
Sylvia and Sam Brenner, New York City
Dorice and Norman Brickman, Menands, New York
Canadian Maccabiah Games Association, Inc.
Mr. and Mrs. Sheldon H. Cloobeck, Encino, California
Harriet and Martin L. Cohen, Teaneck, New Jersey
Selma and Haskell Cohen, Fort Lee, New Jersey
The Terry L. Cole Family, Ventura, California
Mr. and Mrs. Allan Dalfen, Beverly Hills, California
Marilyn and Simon J. Dennenberg, Wynnewood, Pennsylvania
Zofia and Jan Dymant, Harrison, New York
Dagmar and Bob Feldman, Sands Point, New York
Mr. and Mrs. Leon Feldman, Los Angeles, California
Mr. and Mrs. Morris B. Fell, Tulsa, Oklahoma
Mr. Larry Friend, Beverly Hills, California
Edith and Norman Goldbloom, Chevy Chase, Maryland
Mr. Geldalio Grinberg, North American Watch Corporation,
    New York City
Jerome, Jeffrey and Randolf Gumenick, Richmond, Virginia
Yetta and Al Hoffman, Glenview, Illinois
Richard and Lois Hollender, Rockville, Maryland
Paul I. Jacks, Hawthorne, California
Richard M. Kagan, Beverly Hills, California
Mr. and Mrs. Jerome A. Kaplan, Bethesda, Maryland
Jeremy Simon Katzin, South Africa
Mr. Ben Kerner, St. Louis, Missouri
Mr. and Mrs. Robert P. Kogod, Bethesda, Maryland
Mr. Jonathan Kovler, Chicago, Illinois
Tessie and Hyman Krackower, West Palm Beach, Florida
Helen and Nicki Lang, Hampstead, Quebec, Canada
Sam and Sophie Lezell, Margate, Florida
Sal and Rita Lowi, Beverly Hills, California
Shirley Marshal Mazer, Englewood, Ohio

Stephen and Mary Meadow, Merry May Charitable Foundation, Inc.,
    Los Angeles, California
David C. Miller, Philadelphia, Pennsylvania — in memory of
    Charles A. Kahaner
Gerald J. Miller, Silver Springs, Maryland
Ilene and Melvyn K. Miller, Philadelphia, Pennsylvania
Mrs. Phyllis Lowi Miller, Beverly Hills, California
Ross, Jonathan and Alyson Miller, Philadelphia, Pennsylvania
Charlotte and Bernard Mollen, Springfield, New Jersey
Mr. and Mrs. Sidney Morse, Los Angeles, California
Belmont S. and Eva Musicant, Los Angeles, California
Mr. and Mrs. Dennis Needleman, Los Angeles, California
Noreen and Arnold S. Nelson, Beverly Hills, California
Meurice and Ralph Ochsman, Washington, D.C.
Ervin Pfefferman and Son, Los Angeles, California
David and Gerry Pincus, Wynnewood, Pennsylvania
Anita and Benjamin Rabinovitch, Beverly Hills, California
Estherly and Leonard Reifman, Los Angeles, California
Barbara and Don Rickles, Beverly Hills, California
Lt. Col. Louis A. Robbins, Del Rey Beach, Florida
Helen, Stan, and Nicole Roth, Los Angeles, California — in memory of
    Jack J. Sarver, Tucson, Arizona
Mr. and Mrs. Fred Schoenfeld, New York City
Mr. and Mrs. Dan Schusterman, Hal, Stacy, and Jay, Tulsa, Oklahoma
Elsie and Sam Sharrow, Miami Beach, Florida
Claire and Alan Sherman, Bethesda, Maryland
Jeanette and Charles P. Sherman, Washington, D.C.
Marion and Ernest I. Sherman, Chevy Chase, Maryland
Bonnie and Neil Sherman, Potomac, Maryland
Mr. and Mrs. Richard Shostak, Encino, California
Margery Jason Shrinsky, Potomac, Maryland
Bobbie and Joe Siegman, Beverly Hills, California
Ruffy and Evelyn Silverstein, Chicago, Illinois
Mr. and Mrs. Robert H. Smith, Bethesda, Maryland
Robert Spivak and Taylor Hogge, Philadelphia, Pennsylvania
Louise and William Steerman, Gladwyne, Pennsylvania

Dr. Morton and Betty Paul Steuer, South Norwalk, Connecticut
Stonefield and Josephson, Los Angeles, California
Marilyn and Harry Swimmer, Charlotte, North Carolina
Terrel and Zimmelman, Inc., Los Angeles, California
Mr. and Mrs. Bernard Tillipman, Los Angeles, California
Gary Ulrich, Montreal, Canada — in memory of George Wasserman,
     George Wasserman Foundation, Washington, D.C. Wilder Industries,
     Philadelphia, Pennsylvania
Col. and Mrs. Alfred Winograd, New York City
Sam and Teddi Winograd, Beverly Hills, California
Anne and Robert G. Woolf, Boston, Massachusetts
Mr. Michael Yudin, New York City
Judy and Gene Zahn, Beverly Hills, California
David Zinkoff, Philadelphia, Pennsylvania
Mr. Stanley R. Zupnik, Chevy Chase, Maryland

The Tribute program is still active. If you would like to pay tribute to a Hall of Fame honoree of your choice, write for information to: IJSHOF, Wingate Institute, Wingate Post Office, Israel 42902.

THE MUNICH ELEVEN

In the late summer of 1972, at the Olympic Games in Munich, Germany, eleven Israeli athletes were murdered by Arab terrorists.

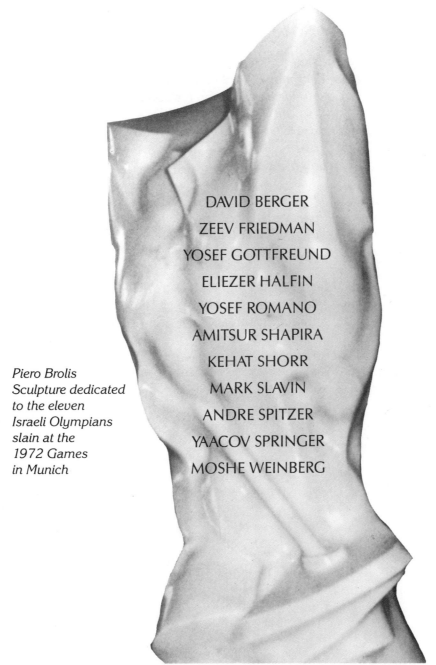

Piero Brolis Sculpture dedicated to the eleven Israeli Olympians slain at the 1972 Games in Munich

DAVID BERGER

ZEEV FRIEDMAN

YOSEF GOTTFREUND

ELIEZER HALFIN

YOSEF ROMANO

AMITSUR SHAPIRA

KEHAT SHORR

MARK SLAVIN

ANDRE SPITZER

YAACOV SPRINGER

MOSHE WEINBERG

Of the many essays of consolation spoken and published throughout the civilized world regarding the atrocity, Wingate Institute (who lost three of its staff members in the horror) published the following poem from the *Ceylon Times,* in its monthly newsletter:

> *Weep tears again;*
> *Hot bitter tears*
> *For Moshe, slain . . .*
>
> *With thousands more like him*
> *Bright, radiant, strong,*
> *He came to speak his word to sing his song;*
> *Bright, radiant, strong, he came*
> *With thousands more like him to play a game.*
>
> *Tell me, I beg you once again,*
> *Tell me*
> *Why was young Moshe slain?*
> *For some ten thousand year old bond of hate?*
> *For some unknown untold caprice of fate?*
> *Or was it as they say because he was Moshe?*
>
> *Poor young Moshe, they'll lay you soon*
> *Into the sand where never sun nor moon,*
> *Where never sound nor light*
> *Will touch your endless night.*
> *How sad young friend, that as they say,*
> *You had to die*
>
> *Because you were Moshe . . .*
>
> *Weep tears again poor world,*
> *Weep tears again,*
> *Hot bitter tears,*
> *For Moshe, slain.*

by Nalini

The International Jewish Sports Hall of Fame's Pillar of Faith is a permanent memorial to the Munich Eleven.